THE DRAGON MAN

BORGO PRESS BOOKS BY BRIAN STABLEFORD

Algebraic Fantasies and Realistic Romances: More Masters of Science Fiction
Changelings and Other Metamorphic Tales
A Clash of Symbols: The Triumph of James Blish
The Cure for Love and Other Tales of the Biotech Revolution
The Devil's Party: A Brief History of Satanic Abuse
The Dragon Man: A Novel
Firefly: A Novel of the Far Future
The Gardens of Tantalus and Other Delusions
Glorious Perversity: The Decline and Fall of Literary Decadence
Gothic Grotesques: Essays on Fantastic Literature
The Haunted Bookshop and Other Apparitions
Heterocosms: Science Fiction in Context and Practice
In the Flesh and Other Tales of the Biotech Revolution
The Innsmouth Heritage and Other Sequels
Jaunting on the Scoriac Tempests and Other Essays on Fantastic Literature
The Moment of Truth: A Novel
News of the Black Feast and Other Random Reviews
An Oasis of Horror: Decadent Tales and Contes Cruels
Opening Minds: Essays on Fantastic Literature
Outside the Human Aquarium: Masters of Science Fiction, Second Edition
Slaves of the Death Spiders and Other Essays on Fantastic Literature
The Sociology of Science Fiction
Space, Time, and Infinity: Essays on Fantastic Literature
The Tree of Life and Other Tales of the Biotech Revolution
Yesterday's Bestsellers: A Voyage Through Literary History

THE DRAGON MAN

A NOVEL OF THE FUTURE

by

Brian Stableford

THE BORGO PRESS

An Imprint of Wildside Press LLC

MMIX

CONTENTS

ABOUT THE AUTHOR

BRIAN STABLEFORD was born in Yorkshire in 1948. He taught at the University of Reading for several years, but is now a full-time writer. He has written many science fiction and fantasy novels, including: *The Empire of Fear, The Werewolves of London, Year Zero, The Curse of the Coral Bride*, and *The Stones of Camelot*. Collections of his short stories include: *Sexual Chemistry: Sardonic Tales of the Genetic Revolution, Designer Genes: Tales of the Biotech Revolution*, and *Sheena and Other Gothic Tales*. He has written numerous nonfiction books, including *Scientific Romance in Britain, 1890-1950, Glorious Perversity: The Decline and Fall of Literary Decadence*, and *Science Fact and Science Fiction: An Encyclopedia*. He has contributed hundreds of biographical and critical entries to reference books, including both editions of *The Encyclopedia of Science Fiction* and several editions of the library guide, *Anatomy of Wonder*. He has also translated numerous novels from the French language, including several by the feuilletonist Paul Féval. Many of his books are being published by the Borgo Press Imprint of Wildside Press.

THE DRAGON MAN

CHAPTER I

When she returned home after the funeral, the first impression that took form in Sara's mind was that everything had happened very quickly, in a mere matter of days. When she had thought about it for a while, though, she realized that her involvement in the Dragon Man's life-story had actually begun some time before she first spoke to him. Their fates had intersected even before she was forced to contact him about the perfume of her rose, and long before she first caught sight of his remarkable face.

Eventually, when she had put all the pieces of the story together, to her own satisfaction, she concluded that the Dragon Man's part in her life-story had begun on her sixth birthday....

* * * * * * *

On her sixth birthday, which fell on the eleventh of July 2374, five of Sara's parents decided at breakfast that they would take her to Blackburn to see the fire fountain in the New Town Square.

Father Lemuel could have come, but he didn't. He went back to his cocoon, saying, as he usually did when he left parental meetings, that he was "going to work," although Sara had once overheard Mother Quilla say that "Lem hasn't done a stroke of real work since he turned a hundred." Father Stephen and Mother Verena both worked away from the hometree somewhere in ManLiv, so they couldn't come. They called their own robocab to take them in the opposite direction.

"Maybe we ought to have called three cabs," Mother Jolene said, as the greater part of the family piled into the Blackburn-bound vehicle. "Five adults and a growing child would be a squeeze even if Steve's legs didn't take up more room than he can possibly need."

Father Stephen was the tallest of Sara's parents, although he wasn't an athlete. When Sara had asked him why, he'd explained to her that he hadn't actually planned to be as tall as he was; he'd just kept on growing a little longer than was fashionable nowadays.

"If all nine of us ever go out together," Mother Maryelle said, in response to Mother Jolene, "we'll have to hire a bus."

"It'll never happen," said Father Aubrey. "Lem comes out of his cocoon to attend house-meetings, but it'll take more than one of Sara's birthdays to get him out of the house."

Sara had overheard more than one of her parents complain about Father Lemuel's "attitude problems". Mother Verena had said only three days before that "Lem only applied to be a parent now because he doesn't want to die without exercising his license." The remark had stuck in Sara's mind, even though she wasn't entirely sure what Mother Verena meant, because she'd been struck by the way that Mother Maryelle's reply had been delivered in the same severe tone that she used whenever she accused Sara of being naughty.

"Without Lem's money," Mother Maryelle had said, "we wouldn't have been able to afford a top-of-the-range hometree in such a good location." Sara wasn't sure why the hometree was so special, although she had been told several times that it was a whole kilometer away from its nearest neighbor.

When the robocab rolled out of the driveway into the lane Sara pressed her face to the window, which was made of transparent plastic and therefore incapable of displaying any other world than the one that was both real and present. All she could see through it was what was actually there, but that was the whole point; the journey was new to her, and she wanted to savor it.

Sara had looked out into the town through the picture window in her bedroom. She had seen the fire fountain that way—but looking through a picture window wasn't the same as being there. She had seen thousands of different places through the window, as many real as virtual, but she couldn't remember having been any further in the flesh than the lanes and fields around the hometree's garden. The last time she had been taken to Blackburn by her parents she had been a baby, unable to take notice of what was happening. She was old enough now to have learned to program the picture window herself, so that she could look out of it at any place in the real world or the virtual multiverse she cared to visit, but seeing the world wasn't the same thing as being able to go there.

Seen through her bedroom window, Blackburn was an uninteresting place by comparison with others Sara had looked at, but the fact that she could actually go there made it a great deal more exciting than any virtual world—even the virtual worlds contained in Father Lemuel's cocoon, which could be touched as well as seen and heard, unlike those she could look into wearing her own hood.

Sara didn't like using the hood to go into virtual worlds, partly because they never seemed quite as real as they appeared to be when seen through her bedroom window, and partly because the hood was what she wore to go to school. Now that she was six she would have to be at school for five hours a day instead of two, for at least another *thirteen years*—which seemed, at present, an eternity.

Blackburn also seemed more exciting, as the robocab turned the corner into the main road, than ManLiv or Manhattan, Morecambe or Madras. All those were places to which she would one day be able to go, if she wanted to, but Blackburn was the one and only place she could go *now*. She was already looking forward to setting foot on the pure white flagstones of New Town Square—which was actually very old now, having been called "New" when the town was rebuilt at the beginning of the twenty-second century, after the Crash. She'd checked it out in her window before running downstairs to join her eager parents, so she knew that the fire fountain stood in the north-western corner of the square, where the Cloistered Facade almost met the Municipal Parade.

Sara didn't want to miss a thing. She wanted to be able to tell her best friend Gennifer all about her excursion, although Gennifer was sure to be unimpressed. Gennifer lived way up north, in Keswick, so she not only had a town right on her doorstep, but a lake called Derwent Water within walking distance.

As the cab accelerated along the road Sara looked back to see if she could still see her hometree. The only visible part of it was the top of the green crown that entitled it to be called a hometree rather than a mere house, and even that soon passed out of sight, giving her a slight thrill of detachment.

The road was like a groove cut into the countryside—which, Sara realized, was why she couldn't see the traffic on it when she opened her bedroom window to look out over the fields beyond the garden hedge. The grass-covered banks to either side were starred with colored flowers, but that seemed a poor substitute for a long view over the fields, taking in facfarms and SAPorchards, other people's hometrees and distant skymasts.

There weren't as many other vehicles on the road as Sara had expected, but they were various in type. She was surprised to observe that only one robocab in three wore the blue-and-silver livery of Blackburn. Her parents never used any other, so all the cabs that had ever come into the hometree's drive had worn those colors, but there were plenty of cabs on the road displaying ManLiv's red-and-sky-blue, and it didn't take long to spot half a dozen other combinations. Some must be from Preston, but she had no idea where the rest might be based.

When Sara looked across at the southbound carriageway, she could see that the cabs there were dutifully flocking together as they coordinated their cruising speeds in the inside lane. The middle lane was the province of trucks, which came in many different shapes and sizes. There were occasional private cars too, but they were mostly uncustomized, as soberly clad as the trucks. The bikes in the outermost lane—the human drivers' lane—were even more brightly-decorated than the cabs, because bikes were what people rode for pleasure rather than purpose. Their riders were more colorful still.

"Bikers put extra surskins on over their smartsuits," Father Aubrey told her, when he noticed that Sara's flickering gaze had begun following the speeding machines on their own northbound carriageway as they zoomed past the cabs and trucks.

"I know," Sara told him. "Ms. Mapledean told us." Ms. Mapledean was her class-teacher.

Father Aubrey frowned slightly, but he went on stubbornly, as if he were determined to find something to tell her that she didn't already know. "Their smartsuits could protect them from the wind perfectly well," he said, "but putting on the extra layer is like putting on a new personality. Bikers love to deck themselves out like birds in fancy plumage—much fancier than those silly things fashionable women in ManLiv have taken to wearing."

"Actually, they're more like wasps displaying warning coloration," Father Stephen put in, while Mother Jolene rolled her eyes in protest against Father Aubrey's insult to "fashionable women".

"They're not like wasps at all," Father Aubrey retorted. "You shouldn't say things that might confuse Sara. It's all about enjoyment—the speed trip."

"There's no need to sound so wistful, Aubie," Mother Quilla said. "If it's what you fancy...."

"I'm a parent now," Father Aubrey said. "There'll be time enough to get back into the fast lane when Sara's grown up."

"Bikers are slugs with delusions of grandeur," Father Gustave observed. "If you want to savor speed, you have to get a power-glider. That really does justify dressing up like a bird and pretending to be a hawk among the sparrows."

THE DRAGON MAN, BY BRIAN STABLEFORD

"Airspeed isn't really speed at all, Gus," Father Aubrey said, hotly. "If you haven't got the ground beneath your wheels, you don't get the sensation of traveling at all."

Sara had tried flying like a bird in virtual space, not just in her hood but in Father Lemuel's cocoon, which was equipped to provide a much better simulation of reality. On that particular occasion the simulation had worked a little too well; she'd felt giddy and more than a little sick. If her Internal Technology hadn't calmed her down she might actually have been sick—which would have annoyed Father Lemuel dreadfully. Father Lemuel wasn't any more prone to annoyance than her other parents, but he was exceedingly fond of his cocoon and the wealth of virtual experience it provided.

The roadside scenery began to improve as the robocab came into the outskirts of the town, where there were walls and hedges with gardens and houses lurking behind. Sara caught fleeting glimpses of glittering walls that were quite unlike the bark-like exterior of her own hometree; hereabouts there were houses that did not try to hide their artificiality behind a vegetal mask, but seemed proud to be carved out of polished stone and roofed in stern jet black.

As the cab moved into denser but less varied traffic, slowing down as it neared the town centre, buildings clustered about the very edge of the road, looming up into the sky. There was an abundance of picture windows close to ground-level, many of them offering displays of goods and services for sale, although most were blank because they could only offer images of virtual worlds to people on the inside. A few offered views of barren deserts and ice-fields, teeming cities or lush forests to any and all passers-by, as if taking care to remind them that Blackburn, like everywhere else on the planet, was part of a Global Village, a Commonwealth of Souls.

Sara would have preferred to leave the cab some distance from the New Town Square and walk along one or two of those fascinating streets, but her parents always seem to be worried about "over-tiring" her. They still seemed to think that she'd only just learned to walk. She had complained about it once to Mother Quilla, who had apologized and explained that it was because parents had no real idea of the rate at which children changed—but it hadn't stopped her. Fortunately the traffic-management system forced the robocab to set them down in the south-eastern corner of the square, so they had a lot of shop-fronts to walk past as they made their way around, many of which were discreetly set back in the slightly mysterious alcoves of the Cloistered Facade.

"Thanks," said Father Gustave, as they all got out. He was speaking to Father Aubrey, who's offered him a supportive hand.

"We aim to please, sir," the cab's Artificial Intelligence replied, automatically. "We hope to have the pleasure of your patronage again."

By the time they got half way along the cloister, Sara had stopped peering into the picture-windows on her right because her eyes had fixed themselves on the prospect ahead—not so much on the fire fountain itself, oddly enough, but on the crowd gathered around it.

The fact that there were twenty-five or thirty adults standing around the fire fountain was uninteresting, so Sara was hardly aware of it. The fact that they had brought their own children was a different matter.

Sara had met hundreds of other children in dozens of different virtual spaces, in addition to the fifteen classmates of her own age who were her regular companions in school. She often played with other children, in the many and various ways that children could play together while they were wearing hoods in their separate rooms. She was perfectly used to being with other children—but the only one she had ever met "in the flesh" was an older boy named Mike whom she had encountered on two occasions, quite by chance, when her parents had taken her for a walk in the countryside surrounding her hometree.

Because Mike and Sara had each been accompanied, on both occasions, by at least four adults, and because they were so obviously not the same age, their meetings had been guarded and wary, and certainly had not involved any actual physical contact. Although Mike attended Sara's school he was two years ahead of her, and had not so far deigned to recognize her during assemblies, break times or club sessions. Sara didn't even know his second name. Now, though, she found herself close—*actually* close—to no less than five other children of assorted ages. They ranged from a babe in arms to a boy twice as tall as Sara, who might have been nine or ten.

It was these other children, rather than the fountain, that drew Sara's eyes. As she approached them, in company with her parental escort, all of them—even the big boy—turned their eyes towards her, with similar curiosity.

* * * * * * *

THE DRAGON MAN, BY BRIAN STABLEFORD

When she recalled this experience at the age of fourteen, after the Dragon Man's funeral, Sara wondered why she hadn't noticed at the time that it wasn't only the children who were looking at her avidly, consumed with curiosity. The simple answer was that her own attention had been too narrowly focused—but there was a little more to it than that.

Six-year-old Sara was accustomed to being the centre of her own parents' attention, so it didn't seem to her that being looked at by adults as anything out of the ordinary. She had been too young, at that time, to realize that there was anything to be noticed, or pondered upon, in the fact that other adults were looking at her too. Children were a different matter. The fact that she could meet their eyes in real space—"meatspace", as Father Lemuel insisted on calling it—had seemed extraordinarily significant.

And so it had been, fourteen-year-old Sara thought. It had been as significant, in its own way, as the shop whose window of which her six-year-old self had not yet caught sight.

CHAPTER II

Sara knew that the other children who had been brought to see the fire fountain that day must all attend the same school she did. Blackburn was not the kind of town that attracted tourists from outside the county. She was surprised, therefore, that she could only put a name to one of them: a girl wearing a pale blue smartsuit not unlike her own. Her name was Samantha Curtyn, and she was eight.

The boy in dark green standing next to Samantha—close enough to touch her, although his hands were at his sides—also seemed to be about eight, but Sara couldn't remember seeing him in school.

It wasn't surprising that Sara couldn't identify the other girl in the crowd, or guess her age, because the part of her smartsuit covering her face wasn't conventionally invisible; it had been temporarily reset to make a cat-like mask, complete with fake whiskers. The second girl was shorter than Samantha Curtyn, and might therefore have been intermediate between her age and Sara's, but there was no way to be sure. Sara felt slightly resentful of the fact that the other girl could almost certainly recognize her, and put a name to her too, without granting a similar privilege to others.

The other boy, whose height marked him out as the oldest, was also clad in unusual finery, but his face was clear; it was only his suit that was tuned up to show off, displaying a slightly dizzying kaleidoscopic effect. She presumed that he didn't wear it that way at home, although she couldn't actually be sure. In school, of course, he would only present an image synthesized by his hood; the sober dress required of that image didn't have to reflect what he was actually wearing.

Sara studied them all, and they studied her. In school, their virtual images would have been equipped with tags, and she would have been able to use her private cursor to click on the tags in order to discover their names, their ages, which classes they were in, where they lived and what their desktop numbers were. Their actual bodies had no such tags, and were therefore intrinsically mysterious.

In school, Sara rarely bothered to click on anyone's tag, unless she had forgotten a name she ought to know, and when she did she never took much notice of the additional information. Because the information was always available, only a click away, it wasn't necessary to commit it to memory. Now that there were no tags available, though, she couldn't help feeling curious about who the other children were and where they had come from.

She knew that her frustration was temporary, and slightly silly. Tomorrow, when she saw these other children in school, she would know that she had met them in the flesh—except for the annoying girl who only had courage enough to venture into the real world if her face was hidden—and they would know that they had met her. They would all be able to click away to their hearts' content, learning everything they wanted to know...but they probably wouldn't feel the need.

* * * * * * *

Remembering the moment fourteen years later, Sara was able to appreciate the paradoxes inherent in her wary observation of the other children more fully than she had at the time.

At six, Sara's awareness of the fact that none of them were likely to become her close friends had been vague and inconsequential. At fourteen, though, she could see a certain irony in the fact that they had been—and were likely to remain—socially distant, even though they lived far closer to her hometree, in meatspace terms, than Gennifer Corcoran, who was the only one of her classmates with whom the six-year-old had regular conversations on camera, desktop-to-desktop.

At fourteen, Sara could see a certain unfortunate perversity in the fact that chance and the whim of the Population Bureau Licensing Authority had ordained that she was to be the only child born within fifty kilometres of her hometree in the year 2367—with the result that none of her classmates lived near enough to make a casual meeting in real space likely. And she knew, at fourteen, that no such meeting had yet occurred—nor would it, without a great deal of preparation and careful interparental negotiation.

* * * * * * *

THE DRAGON MAN, BY BRIAN STABLEFORD

Thanks to the presence of the other children and their reaction to six-year-old Sara's arrival in the square, the fire fountain went almost unheeded by its audience for a full three minutes. Those who had been brought to marvel at its display were too busy marveling at one another.

When Sara did try to focus on the fountain, she found it quite uninteresting by comparison. Some trick of perspective made it seem smaller now than it had when she had stared at it through her bedroom window, and the fact that the sparks did not seem substantial, or even warm, when they drifted far enough from their source to land on her head and shoulders was strangely disappointing. They should have seemed more real, given that she was actually there, but they didn't.

Even when you were standing right next to it, Sara realized, the fire fountain was just a special effect.

For that reason, the fact that the fountain was doing what it did in real space rather than virtual space didn't seem half as significant as the fact that the other children were actually present, rather than being images carved in light. The sparks jetting forth from the fountain to follow dozens of strange trajectories weren't real sparks at all. They were only bits of light. They weren't hot; when they landed on someone, they simply winked out of existence, leaving no trace behind of their brief existence. The children, on the other hand, were people. They were solid, intelligent flesh.

That was why it only required two minutes more for Sara's attention to wander again.

It was then that she caught a glimpse, out of the corner of her eye, of the Dragon Man's shop window.

* * * * * * *

Looking back, eight years later, Sara wondered why her six-year-old self had been so abruptly captivated by that glimpse, when she couldn't have been certain of what it was that she was looking at. She remembered that she had stared for thirty seconds or so at the golden dragon that formed the centerpiece of the display before it had dawned on her that the window, like the window of the robocab, really was a window and not a screen pretending to be a window.

Had that really seemed significant, at the time?

No, not significant. Just odd—but odd enough to command a long, hard look.

THE DRAGON MAN, BY BRIAN STABLEFORD

* * * * * * *

Sara realized, belatedly, that she wasn't looking through the eye of a camera at a rather poor three-dimensional visualization of a dragon in flight. She was looking through a plate of clear plastic at a rather fine two-dimensional picture of a dragon in flight: a dragon whose scales were golden on top and silver beneath, with a head like....

She couldn't find anything with which to compare that head among the ranks of living mammals, birds, and reptiles, nor among the much more extensive ranks of the extinct mammals, birds, and reptiles she had seen in virtual reproduction. There was something dog-like about the jaw and brow, something pig-like about the ears, something lizard-like about the teeth and something hawk-like about the eyes, but the head was no haphazard compound. It had its own integrity and its own identity, in spite of being fabulous.

Was it a painting? she wondered. Was it inscribed on paper, or polished stone? She wasn't sure.

Sated by the glory of the dragon, Sara refocused her gaze to take account of the rest of the window-display—which, because the window was only transparent plastic, had to be composed of actual objects.

There were instruments of several different shapes and sizes, many with cables dangling or inartistically coiled, whose purpose she could not begin to grasp, although she could see easily enough that what Father Stephen would have called "the business end" of each device was something like a tiny drill...or a needle.

* * * * * * *

Looking back from the age of fourteen, Sara could not remember how much of what her six-year-old self had seen had been immediately or eventually understandable. Because she understood it so well now, she could not tell how much she had added to the preserved memory as a result of subsequent research.

She did not doubt, though, that there had been an immediately-perceptible strangeness about the window that was even more profound and remarkable than the sight of the five children.

* * * * * * *

Sara tugged Mother Quilla's arm, and said: "What's that, Mother Quilla?"

Mother Quilla turned—and Sara noticed that her other four parents immediately turned too, obedient to her curiosity.

"It's supposed to be a dragon," Mother Quilla said.

"I know that," Sara said. "But what sort of shop is it? Why does it have a painting in the window instead of a virtual display?"

"That's the Dragon Man's shop," said Mother Maryelle. "It's been here much longer than I can remember—maybe since the square was new. It's an antique in its own right."

"Yes," Sara said, "but what sort of shop is it?"

"He's just a tailor, really, much like any other tailor," said Mother Jolene.

"No, he's not," said Father Aubrey. "He doesn't do regulation smartsuits, the way Linda Chatrian does. It's all fancy work. Sublimate technology, isn't that what they call it? Moving pictures. Spiders—that sort of thing."

"Biker gear," Father Gustave put in.

"Flyer gear too," Father Aubrey was quick to retort. "But that's not what Sara means. The Dragon Man's very old, Sara. He was a decorator of sorts long before there were smartsuits to decorate—but in those days tailors were people who dealt in dead clothes. The Dragon Man never sold clothes. He worked on skin, so he wouldn't have been thought of as a tailor at all. He was a tattooist, before the art became redundant. As Maryelle says, that display's probably been there for two hundred years—his own private monument. He's still open for business, though. No second pre-childhood for him."

"Don't be silly, Aubie," Mother Maryelle said. "She's only six. How's she supposed to follow all that?"

Even though she hadn't understood everything that Father Aubrey had said, Sara felt free to be offended by Mother Maryelle's assumption that she wouldn't be able to follow it. She knew, for instance, that Father Aubrey's reference to "a second pre-childhood" was an insult aimed at Father Lemuel's habit of spending at least twenty-three hours a day in his cocoon, living his whole life—except for house-meetings and the occasional meal, which didn't really qualify as "life"—in Virtual Space. What she didn't know was what a "tattooist" was, or why one might be likened to a modern tailor even though he hadn't been one. Alas, she wasn't able to ask, because the adult conversation had already flowed on, as it so often did, acquiring the kind of mad momentum that made certain parental conversations impossible to interrupt.

"Lem used to know him, didn't he?" said Mother Quilla.

"Who?" asked Mother Jolene.

"Frank Warburton," said Mother Quilla.

"Who's Frank Warburton?" asked Father Aubrey.

"The Dragon Man," said Mother Maryelle.

"Everybody knows the Dragon Man," said Mother Jolene.

"*I* know Frank Warburton," said Father Gustave, at the same time as Mother Quilla was saying, "I mean, knew him *personally*," and Mother Maryelle was saying, "Nobody really *knows* the Dragon Man—how can they?" After which, all five of them were trying to speak at once, aiming their remarks in every possible direction but Sara's. She had to wait for her chance to break in on them.

When the chance finally came, Sara said: "What do you mean by *work on skin*? A smartsuit is a sort of skin, isn't it? A surskin."

"The Dragon Man's very old," Father Aubrey repeated, as if he thought that Sara hadn't been listening the first time. "When he started work, people still wore dead clothes...well, clothes that you had to put on in the morning and take off at night, and change in between if you wanted to look different. Some of them were pretty smart, maybe smart enough to be thought of as alive...."

"You're confusing her again," Mother Quilla broke in, accusingly. "It's not so very different nowadays, Sara. We still wear clothing; it's just that over the years...the centuries...our clothing has come to resemble a new outer layer—which is why smartsuits are sometimes called surskins. Yours is so versatile that it grows along with you, and you probably won't have to change it more than two or three times in your lifetime, unless there's a big leap forward in the technology, although you'll start adding new accessories to it once you're in your teens, and keep on adding more and more as you get older...."

"Especially if you're *fashion-conscious*," Father Stephen put in, making it sound like an insult.

"Which you probably will be," Mother Jolene said, giving Father Stephen another dark look, "if you take after me, or Verena, instead of...."

"*To answer Sara's question*," Mother Maryelle broke in, in her most commanding voice, "what Mr. Warburton used to do, a very long time ago, was make pictures in people's skin. Their natural skin, that is."

"You mean, "Sara said, carefully, "that he was a kind of painter."

"No," said Mother Maryelle. "He used a motorized needle, to drive the ink into the skin, so that it would be permanently integrated into it—in much the same way that the colors and textures of your smartsuit are built into it, but much more crudely."

Sara knew that she had to get in quickly if she wanted to remind her parents about her other question before they started bickering again, so she said: "So the dragon isn't a painting, then? It's *inside somebody's skin?*"

Strangely enough, that precipitated a moment's silence before Father Gustave—who liked to think of himself as a natural diplomat, capable of handling the touchiest situations—said: "No, Sara. That dragon in the window is only a hundred and fifty years old or thereabouts. About the same age as Father Lemuel, I think. It's inscribed on—or in—synthetic skin. It's not from an actual person."

"Oh," said Sara, trying as hard as she could to present the appearance of the highly intelligent, sophisticated child that all eight of her parents so obviously wanted her to be. "I see."

* * * * * * *

On many an occasion, in the years that followed, Sara had thought that it must have been a great deal easier to be a child in the days before the Crash, when all parental conversations had been two-way, and even seven- or eight- or nine-year-olds must have stood a fair-to-middling chance of interrupting. Once five adults—let alone the eight who gathered at house-meetings—began talking at cross purposes, the task of restoring order required a much more powerful voice than that of the tiny creature whose care and education had brought them all together in the first place.

Two parents, fourteen-year-old Sara thought, couldn't possibly have put as much pressure on a six-year-old child as eight, even if they had entertained such high expectations. In the days when children only had two parents, of course, genetic engineering hadn't been sufficiently advanced to make certain that all children were highly intelligent—but the combined expectations of eight parents, Sara now understood, were massive enough to outweigh any advantage conferred by science.

At six—and, indeed, at every other age she had passed through on her arduous journey to the present—Sara had always felt that she had been lagging behind, not yet capable of being the child her parents wanted and expected her to be. When, exactly, had she begun to wonder whether it was her parents that might be asking too much rather than she who might be failing? Was it before or after she had first defied them in a flagrant and spectacular fashion by climbing the hometree? Or was it, perhaps, climbing the hometree that had brought the long-held suspicion to the surface? She didn't know. She couldn't remember.

What she did know, and could remember, was that when her six-year-old self had gone home on the day of her sixth birthday, after a short walk through the streets of Blackburn, during which a hundred other things had been pointed out to her by five eager index fingers, the one enduring image that her mind had retained was the golden dragon. That image had somehow succeeded in seeming more interesting, and more precious, than the momentary presence of the other children.

In retrospect, Sara could see that the brief glimpse of the dragon within the cloister had been the only aspect of the experience that had actually started something: a chain of ideas and actions that had run, unsteadily but unbroken, all the way to the day when she actually entered that mysterious shop, in order to confront the exotic creature whose lair it was.

CHAPTER III

Even at six, Sara had been old enough to look up "tattoos" with the aid of her desktop. She still had enough curiosity left when she returned home on that birthday to try.

Unfortunately, the torrent of information released by her enquiry had too much in it that was impenetrably confusing. What did "sublimate technology" mean? Why were its products sometimes called "astral tattoos" if they weren't tattoos at all? What had "military tattoos" got to do with it? The questions were too awkward—and the information which didn't raise questions seemed, for the most part, rather repulsive.

Dragons, on the other hand, were easy for the six-year-old mind to get a grip on, and considerably more fascinating than tattoos. The most immediate legacy of Sara's first trip into town, therefore, was a interest in dragons which became intense for a matter of months and lingered within her for years afterwards.

In Father Stephen's room, which housed the most prized items of his collection of pre-Crash junk, six-year-old Sara found two statuettes formed in the image of dragons. One was made of plastic, the other of glass. He gave her the plastic one immediately, when she expressed an interest, but he told her the other was too fragile. He obviously felt guilty about keeping it, though, because he gave her a bag full of old CDs and diskettes and volunteered to take her to the next junk swap in Old Manchester, so that she could go dragon-hunting on her own behalf.

Sara's excitement at Father Stephen's gift was only slightly muted when Father Lemuel asked to have a look at the contents of the bag. "I know that the word *junk* is supposed to have been stripped of all its pejorative connotations, Steve," he said, talking over Sara's head, "but this stuff really is junk. She won't get anything much in exchange for this rubbish."

"That's where you're wrong," Father Stephen said. "I wouldn't get much for it, because I'd be bartering on level terms—but Sara only has to smile sweetly, and every carpet-trader in St Anne's Square will be only too willing to give her model dragons in exchange for any old rubbish she has to trade. Plastic ones, anyway."

"That's exploitation!" Mother Quilla objected.

"No it's not," Father Stephen retorted. "It would be exploitation if I were asking her to barter on my behalf for things I wanted—which certain parents in ManLiv are only too happy to do—but if she's bartering on her own behalf she's perfectly entitled to take advantage of her opportunities. I'm just furthering her education."

After that, the argument became heated and quite impenetrable, but Sara found out soon enough that what Father Stephen had said was true. Children did have a tremendous advantage at junk swaps, where even the traders who had so little regard for etiquette that they would take credit seemed absolutely delighted that a child so young could take an interest in their collections. They were so enthusiastic to welcome her to the community of junkies—or "Preservers of the Heritage of the Lost World," as they preferred to call themselves—that they would have let her give them anything at all in exchange for ordinary items to which they were not sentimentally attached. In effect, they were giving them to her, and gladly—but junkie etiquette demanded that some exchange of goods should take place, no matter how contrived. And how else could she learn to be a good junkie?

By taking advantage of her youth and Father Stephen's seemingly-infinite supply of junk so rubbishy that he "couldn't swap it for dust" Sara soon built up a collection of dragons modelled in several kinds of plastic. She also acquired a fine set of old paperback books with pictures of dragons on the covers, including a few that would have been quite valuable if the pages hadn't been so badly acid-burned that they splintered into fragments if they were turned.

Although she hardly qualified as a "real junkie" Sara was infected by the glamour of the past to the extent that she prized the figurines and paperback covers more than the whole dragon-filled worlds that could be conjured up on the other side of her bedroom window, or visited by means of her hood. Throughout her seventh and eight years she tuned her window to dragonworlds more often than not, but there was a magic in fondling the pre-Crash fabrications that mere sightseeing could not provide.

In addition to five junk swaps, Sara's parents took her out into the world beyond the garden fence on five more occasions before her seventh birthday arrived, and even more regularly thereafter, but whenever destinations were discussed, the fire fountain was always dismissed as something already seen and done. She could have asked to go back to New Town Square, but she never did. The golden dragon was always available to her in virtual space, and she felt no urgent need to look at it even there.

By the time her tenth birthday rolled around Sara had been back and forth from Blackburn nearly twenty times. She had been to hospital twice to be scanchecked, and twice more to add new colonies of nanobots to her Internal Technology. On other excursions, she went shopping for various "hometree improvements", and visited the family's tailor, Linda Chatrian—whose fitting-rooms were only forty metres away from the south-eastern corner of New Town Square—in order to ensure that the growth of her smartsuit kept pace with her body's maturation.

She had also been to half a dozen different playcenters in the town, although she had always felt slightly out of place there because there was never anyone else from her own birth-year. Sara preferred going south to playcenters in the ManLiv Corridor, where she was able to meet some of her classmates in the flesh, including Davy Bennett, Leilah Nazir and Margareta Madrovic. None of these real world acquaintances ever threatened to replace Gennifer Corcoran as her best friend, even though Gennifer lived way up north in Keswick, but it was good to see them in an environment where they walked and ran and stumbled in a refreshingly clumsy way, rather than floating through virtual space in response to the instructions of hidden cursors.

Between the ages of six and fourteen Sara passed dozens of personal milestones marking out the phases of her youth, but when she looked back on them all the one that seemed to be the most important of all was the day not long after her tenth birthday when she climbed the hometree. It was important not merely because it was the first time she had defied her parents so blatantly, but because it was the first time she had ever been truly afraid. She could not have been nearly as proud of herself had it not been for the magical combination of those two factors.

Looking back four years later, Sara understood that climbing the hometree could not have been very difficult. She had had to wait until she was unobserved long enough to get a good head start of Mother Quilla and Mother Verena, who were on garden watch that particular day, but once she had evaded their attention for two or three minutes she was well out of reach, clambering up the side of the house far too rapidly to be overtaken. The speed of her ascent was evidence not only of the abundance of hand- and foot-holds but of their firmness; she had never been in any real danger of slipping and falling—but it had not seemed that way at the time. At the time, she had felt that she was doing something difficult and dangerous, something fabulously daring. Had she not been so fearful, she could not have been so excited.

It was not the first forbidden thing Sara had ever done, and perhaps not even the naughtiest, but it was the one that carried her to the greatest height.

Mother Quilla spotted her while Sara was still clambering up the outer face of the second storey, but it was too late by then.

"Sara! Come down at once!" was Mother Quilla's entirely expectable reaction, but Sara simply ignored her. Mother Verena actually ran to the wall and tried to set off after her, but found out soon enough what Sara had already realized: that the nooks and crannies in the bark finish offered plenty of toeholds to someone of her size, but far fewer to adult feet. Mother Verena, who was not one of nature's quitters, even attempted to modify her smartsuit to simulate bare feet instead of gardening boots, but that only meant that she howled with pain when she had to jump back down again, having attained a height no more than a couple of metres off the ground.

"If you don't come down *this minute* you'll be under house arrest for the next six months!" Mother Quilla threatened—but Sara wasn't to be intimidated. Within the house she had the Virtual Space of the entire Global Village at her disposal, not to mention hundreds of Fantasylands, but the chance to climb to the top of the hometree in the flesh wasn't likely to come again any time soon, now that she had revealed the ambition. She kept going.

As seen from ground level, the hometree her parents had bought in order to provide a home for Sara was not so very different from a town house. It was rectangular in section, and it had a perfectly ordinary front door. It had windows on every side, big ones on the ground floor and slightly smaller ones on the first and second floors—none of which were picture-windows when viewed from the outside, so that they all looked uniformly grey when they weren't tuned to transparency. Given all that, the "bark finish" on the walls wasn't going fool anyone into thinking that they were really looking at a tree, rather than a house with tree-like decor. The roots of the house's biosystems were, of course, invisible.

Even if one looked up at it from the ground—at least from Sara's meager height—the top of the hometree didn't look so very different from the decorated roofs of many stone-effect town houses, because its complexity wasn't obvious at that range. It was evident that the crown had leaves, but they seemed to merge together into a kind of green fuzz whose shape was unclear, and the internal structure of the crown—the branches and their emergence from the attics above the third-storey ceilings—was hidden.

Seen from within, on the other hand, the hometree's crown was a realm of marvels.

Once she was in the crown, the climbing became so absurdly easy that Sara felt sure that there was no longer any danger of her falling, at least until she tried to clamber down again. There were sturdy branches aplenty, offering abundant handholds and secure footholds. The crown was tall, more like a steeple than a poplar, let alone an oak, but Sara did not feel that she was unsafe even when the combination of her weight and the breeze made it stir and sway.

She had expected to see birds in the branches of the tree, because she often heard their songs from the garden, but the birds themselves all flew away; what she actually saw was their nests—dozens of them, all but a few empty now, though one or two still contained fat chicks sounding shrill alarms. She had not expected so many creepy-crawlies, but every time she reached out for a new handhold things with lots of legs went scurrying away, and things with wings took to the air, some of them large enough to whirr or buzz—and still there were others left to squish beneath her fingers.

By this time, Mother Quilla had summoned help, but Sara could no longer see how many of her parents had come out into the garden, and had to rely on the sounds of their voices to count the witnesses to her daring.

She heard Father Gustave saying, "She'll be quite safe if you don't shout at her. She won't fall unless you scare her into it," and agreed with him wholeheartedly—but that didn't stop Father Stephen lending his stentorian tones to the chorus of disapproval.

"Come down at once, Sara!" he shouted, louder than anyone else—but even his long legs and far-reaching arms weren't up to the task of finding cracks big enough to serve as handholds and footholds while he hauled himself up to attic level.

She heard Mother Maryelle saying, "All kids do it," in the weary way that Mother Maryelle always had when she was pretending that, because she had recently turned a hundred, she had to know more about the business of parenting than those members of the household who had not yet clocked up their first century. She didn't have to hear the drowned-out protests of Father Aubrey and Mother

Jolene to know that they were not in the least consoled by the universality of her mission. Nor was she—she would have preferred to believe that what she was doing was exceptional, if not actually unprecedented.

After that, though, Sara stopped listening to the voices down below, in order to concentrate her attention outwards, at the vast panorama visible from within the high canopy.

It was then that the real fear hit her, and hit her hard.

Sara had never imagined that she was, or could be, afraid of heights. After all, she had often tuned her picture window to views from mountain-tops. She had looked out from similar heights within her hood, both in and out of school. She had even used the hood to "fly" through fabulous skies, pretending that she was a bird or a dragon, or Father Gustave on a powerglider, although the experience hadn't been very convincing. She had experienced vertigo, and had trained her Internal Technology to blank out its symptoms and restore her calm of mind.

But this was different. This time, she knew that she was in real space rather than virtual space, and that the distance between her and the ground was a space through which she could actually fall.

It was meatspace, and she was meat. If she did fall, she would fall like any other piece of meat. Although her smartsuit was armor of a sort, it couldn't protect her from all the kinds of damage that an impact with the ground would inflict. Her Internal Technology would help her flesh to repair itself, but it wouldn't take away all her pain because pain was a warning and had to be allowed to sound its alarm.

If she fell, it would hurt.

If she fell, she'd *be* hurt.

Because she knew all this, Sara's experience was quite different from the experience of looking through a picture window or soaring in virtual space. This vertigo swamped the calming efforts of her IT, and left her giddy with terror.

It was all slightly absurd. She was surrounded by so many branches that it would have been far more difficult to fall than cling on. She knew that, too—but the terror possessed her nevertheless, while long seconds ticked by...and she actually began to believe, if only for a moment, that her parents were right, and that she really ought to do exactly what they said at all times, even if they couldn't always agree among themselves as to what that might be.

CHAPTER IV

Mercifully, the effect was temporary. Whether it was her Internal Technology catching up with its duty, or merely her own consciousness adapting to the situation, the terror drained away. Sara became confident that she could not and would not fall, and that she was free to enjoy the view.

Terror was swiftly replaced by triumph, as she realized what a victory she had won. She had conquered her fear. She had conquered the hometree. She had conquered the brief anxiety that her parents might, after all, be right about *everything.*

The roofs of Blackburn were invisible from the open window of her bedroom, even if she stood on a chair, but from the crown of the hometree Sara could not only see the town sprawled across an improbably tiny section of the north-western horizon, but two other accumulations of dwellings nestling in the hills to the east. She felt slightly ashamed that she could not put a name to either of them, although she knew that the trees clustered between them were the New Forest of Rossendale—which, like the New Town Square, was only as New as the Aftermath of the Crash.

She wished, belatedly, that she had taken the trouble to consult a map before embarking on her climb. Was the ManLiv corridor closer in the south than the sea was in the west? She could not see either of them, not even Preston, which lay between Blackburn and the Ribble Estuary. She could not guess how far behind the south-western horizon the city might be, or the ruins of Old Manchester in the south-east.

She was surprised by the number of black patches littering the landscape, and by the manner in which they were aggregated around buildings which she took to be facfarms. Black was the color of SAP—the Solid Artificial Photosynthesis technology that "fixed" sunlight more efficiently than nature's chlorophyll—but the illustrations posted in her virtual classroom always showed vast tracts laid out in the tropic regions that had once been scorched deserts, never little clusters in the grey-lit Lancashire hills. These were SAPor-chards, not SAPfields. There were green fields too, though, some of them speckled with amber seed-heads and others stained yellow by oilseed rape. The green meadows provided ranges for ground-nesting birds and free-grazing sheep, while the cultivated fields pro-duced animal feed.

She counted no less than nine skymasts on the horizon, some of them lavishly embellished with dishes, but there were no windmills, and no pylons carrying overhead power-lines, such as she had seen in picture window views of the Yorkshire side of the Pennines and the highlands of Scotland. The hometree's electricity was carried by underground cables—which was why it had taken Powerweb so long to locate the break that had left her parents reliant on its feeble inbuilt biogenerator for nearly a week in the depths of the previous winter, causing her to miss four whole days of school.

There were fewer visible roads than Sara had expected, and for a moment or two she wondered whether this was because many of them were so deeply sunken as to be hidden even from this lofty viewpoint—but she realized eventually that, although the world seemed be mostly made of roads while you were traveling in a robo-cab, there was a lot more territory in between them than their claus-trophobic banks allowed passengers to perceive. She was surprised how tiny the vehicles appeared to be—even the greatest of the lum-bering trucks—and how exceedingly tiny the distant people seemed who could be seen walking in the vicinity of the facfarms. It was not until she had noticed them that she realized how vast the country was—and how vast the whole country must be, against whose back-cloth on a map Blackburn and ManLiv seemed to lie almost cheek by jowl.

But the vastest thing of all was the sky. Sara had not expected the sky to seem different, no matter how high she climbed, because it was, after all, an absence rather than a presence, whose emptiness could hardly be increased—but she realized now how little of the sky she had been able to see from the ground, where there were looming objects all around.

From the crown of the hometree, the vastness of the sky was in-creased in proportion to the vastness of the horizon, and she saw for the first time how full of flyers it was—not birds, which were far too tiny to be perceptible much beyond the limits of the garden, but gliders and powergliders, jethoppers, and airships.

31

Sara had already taken due note of the play of color on the roads, and the manner in which the insectile dots that were bright-clad bikers zoomed so easily past the drab trucks, but now she took note of the massed traffic of the air, where there was nothing drab at all. Even the gasbags of the stateliest airships shone luminously silver, while the individual human flyers were as brightly clad as hummingbirds, or tropical butterflies...or fanciful dragons.

After a few moments of turning her head to scan the west from north to south, and then the east from north to south, she realized that there were not so many flyers as she had first thought. They were more thinly distributed than she had assumed, all aggregated within a few degrees of arc about the far horizon—but even so, she could not recall ever having had more than two or three simultaneously in view before, and now she had at least thirty.

She knew that she was not on top of the world by any means, and that the distant Pennine peaks were far more loftily set than the crown of her hometree, but still she felt taller than she had ever felt before—taller than any mere adult. But she knew, too, that when she got back down to ground level she would be just as short as she had been before she started to climb, and that all eight of her absurdly tall parents would be coming down on her hard.

That thought caused another quiver of panic, but it subsided very quickly. Now that she had known real fear, she was not about to be disturbed by something as silly as that. Even so, she took great care while she made her descent, making absolutely sure that she would not give her waiting patents any further cause for concern.

That evening, there was a special house meeting to decide what had to be done about Sara climbing the house. It wasn't the first time a special meeting had been called, nor was it the first parental meeting in which the whole discussion was devoted to arguments about how best to fit a punishment to a crime, but it was different nevertheless, because it was the first time Sara had ever gone into such a meeting in a defiant mood. It wasn't just that she didn't feel ashamed at having climbed nearly to the top of the hometree's crown when she'd been forbidden to do it, but that she felt too much delight in her achievement to worry about any reprisals that her parents were likely to dream up. She expected to be punished, but she was determined to bear her punishment stoically. She also expected to have to face up to a rare unanimity of disapproval and purpose on the part of her eight parents—but that wasn't quite the way it worked out.

THE DRAGON MAN, BY BRIAN STABLEFORD

"What's all the fuss about?" Father Lemuel demanded, almost as soon as Mother Maryelle—whose turn it was to act as chairperson—had called the meeting to order.

"We all know how testy you get when you're dragged out of Fantasyland, Lem," Father Gustave said, "but it really is important. What Sara did was dangerous. If she'd fallen, she could have been killed."

"That's not really the point at issue," Father Stephen put in. "It's a matter of disobedience—a point of principle."

"No it's not," said Mother Quilla. "Obedience isn't a principle. Sara shouldn't do what we say simply because we say it. It's a matter of trust. The principle is whether Sara trusts our judgment in regard to acceptable risk."

"That certainly isn't a principle," Father Gustave objected, scornfully. "Not that it matters a jot one way or the other. Principles don't have anything to do with it. It's purely a matter of making things clear, of explaining to Sara why she shouldn't do things like that."

"Which is a matter of trust, just as Quill says," Mother Jolene put in. She has to realize that we have good reasons for telling her what to do and what not to do, even if they aren't...."

Sara assumed that Mother Jolene was about to say "obvious", but it didn't really matter, because Father Stephen cut her off before she finished the sentence—and Sara had had plenty of opportunity to observe that as soon as one parent took it upon himself, or herself, to interrupt one of the others before a sentence was finished, the rules of polite conversation immediately fell apart. Everybody would then start talking at once—as, indeed, they did.

Two or three minutes elapsed before Mother Maryelle resorted to banging the table with the claw-hammer that had served as a temporary gavel ever since the real one had been mislaid three years earlier. Sara immediately began counting the blows. A five bang row was about average, a ten-bang row exceptional, and a twenty-bang row was likely to lead to talk of divorce. This one turned out to be a twelve-bang row.

"I would have thought," Mother Maryelle said, when she had finally restored silence, "that this was one issue on which we could present a united front. There's no point in arguing about why we're angry...."

"We're not angry," Mother Verena said, getting the comment in an instant before Mother Maryelle started her next sentence, so that it didn't quite qualify as a fully-fledged interruption.

"We're anxious," said Mother Jolene.

"Fearful," said Father Aubrey.

"Concerned," was Father Stephen's offering.

A single bang of the claw-hammer was all it took to put a stop to that sort of trickle.

"*The point*," Mother Maryelle said, her voice consumed by the acid authority that came with the chairperson's job, "is to decide what to do about our...can we call it a disturbance? Is there anyone who can't agree that we're *disturbed* by what happened?"

For half a second, it actually seemed that the compromise might hold—but then Father Lemuel said: "I can't."

This time, it didn't need an interruption for everyone to start talking at once.

Sara observed, not without a certain disturbance of her own, that the discussion had now escalated—or perhaps deteriorated—into a fourteen-bang row.

"All right," Mother Maryelle said, when she had won silence for a second time. From now on, it's one at a time. If we can't manage it without help, I'll get the snowing globe."

The snowing globe was a pre-Crash antique which Father Stephen had given Mother Maryelle for her hundredth birthday—having acquired it, of course, at a junk swap in Old Manchester. Whenever her turn to be chairperson came around, Mother Maryelle controlled disputes that got out of hand by stating the three fundamental rules that the person holding the snowing globe was the only one who could speak, that the person holding the snowing globe had the sole authority to decide who to pass it on to when he or she had finished, and that anyone who ever broke the snowing globe would forfeit a month's wages to the household pool.

After ten seconds of silence, Mother Maryelle said. "Right. Lem, would you care to explain why you can't agree that we're all disturbed by Sara's antics?"

"Perfectly natural thing to do," Father Lemuel said, dismissively. "Had to happen sooner or later. Glad she's got the guts. Lot of fuss about nothing."

Mother Maryelle already had the claw-hammer raised, ready to bring it down if anyone spoke before she gave them leave. "Jo," she said.

"I really do think it's a matter of trust," Mother Jolene said. "Sara did something we told her not to do, and she carried on doing it while we were telling her to stop. She obviously has no faith in our judgment and our reasoning—and that's serious."

Sara knew even before Mother Maryelle's gaze had swept around the whole table that it was going to flick back to her.

"I trusted myself," she said, as firmly as she could. "I trusted myself not to fall—and once I was in the crown, even though I was a little bit scared, it would have been harder to fall than hang on. It was easy. I just wanted to do it—to have a look around. If you want to punish me, that's okay."

"Gus," said Mother Maryelle, quickly.

"It was dangerous, Sara," Father Gustave said, soberly. "It frightened all of us as well as you—except Lem, apparently. It made us anxious, not just about the possibility that you might fall and hurt herself, which thankfully didn't happen, but about this whole project, this whole enterprise."

"That's a bit strong!" Mother Jolene put in, before Mother Maryelle's glare silenced her.

"Is it?" Father Gustave went on. "I'm well over a hundred years old now, Jo, and this is the first time I've ever been a parent. We might all have another chance some day, if Internal Technology continues to improve, but the longer we live, the harder it will become to get licenses, so everyone here has to work on the assumption that this is our one and only chance to raise a child. Even if it weren't, the prospect of failure would be too much to bear. We'll only be living together for twenty or twenty-five years, but if we do the job right, we'll be parents until we die, no matter how widely we scatter when Sara goes her own way. There's a lot at stake here—so we're entitled to be frightened. We're entitled to be terrified by the possibility of failure, of disaster, even if Lem thinks that makes us overprotective. We don't know how long Sara might live; if you trust the ads the IT people put out, she might live to be a thousand; if not—and it's going take a long time before anyone can be sure—she might only have three or four hundred years...*barring accidents*. But I don't think Sara understands, as yet, what kind of risks she's running when she invites the possibility of accidents. I think we need to try harder to make it clear to her. That's what we need to do—what we need to decide."

Ordinarily, Sara would have switched off half way through a speech as long as that, but the day's excitement was making her unusually alert, thus helping to maintain her concentration. "Lem," said Mother Maryelle, swiftly. "Have you got any objection to *that*?"

"Of course I have," Father Lemuel said. "We can't let our fears shape Sara's life—no, cancel that, it's precisely because we can that we have to take care. We *shouldn't* let our fears shape Sara's life. Of course we're scared of being shown up as lousy parents. Even I'd have to live far longer with the shame of having messed it up than I could bear. But it's not her business to calm our fears—it's our business to calm hers, which we won't do by coming down on her hard if she ever steps out of line. She's only a child, granted—but she's not an idiot. She knows she took a risk when she climbed up to the roof. If she'd fallen, she'd have hurt herself. But she watches TV. She rides robocabs. She knows full well that there are people who take much greater risks for the thrill of it, day by day. She knows that there are people sitting at this table who've been bikers, flyers, skiers...I don't suppose she has any real notion of what each of us did for a living before we applied for our license, or what those of us who are still working do, but if she did she'd know that at least half of us have taken measurable risks on an everyday basis in the past, and that at least two of us are still taking measurable risks even now. Okay, we're a boring bunch, on the whole—not a single extreme sportsperson among us—but not one of us would ever have refused on our own behalf the kind of risk that Sara took today, *in the grounds of her own home, while half a dozen of her parents watched.* So I say that if this is a test of some kind, Sara's passed it; we're the ones who are in danger of failing. If we over-react, we fail. Why not just tell her that she scared us—which she must have realized by now—and ask her to be careful, please, to think hard before she scares us like that again?"

Sara was tempted to applaud, but that would have been one impertinence too many. Mother Maryelle had the claw-hammer raised and ready, but this time she had to bring it down to stop three simultaneous protests. "This is obviously going to be harder than we thought," she said, ominously. "Quilla."

Sara immediately guessed what would happen next. She understood that Mother Maryelle's comment had been a hint, which Mother Quilla was expected to take up. Mother Quilla did, immediately proposing a motion that the meeting should be held "in camera"—which meant, in simple terms, that Sara should be sent to bed while her parents got on with the serious business of tearing into one another without her inhibiting presence.

Father Stephen seconded the motion—but Father Lemuel was, for once, unstoppable. "No," he said. "That's the cowards' way out. She's old enough to hear us, now."

For two or three minutes, Sara was immensely pleased by that compliment, and by the fact that in the hectic discussion that followed the original motion was eventually forgotten, and never even put to the vote. After two or three hours, however, she realized that no privilege came without penalties, and that that the privilege of listening to her parents argue about what they should and shouldn't say and do in front of her—especially while she was alert to every word—was a very dubious one indeed.

Eventually, Sara decided that Father Lemuel hadn't said the half of it when he'd observed that they were a boring bunch *on the whole*. Individually, there were only one or two who could have bored for England, but collectively....

The meeting went on for a *very* long time, and got nowhere. By the time Sara did get to her room, free to collapse on her bed, she felt that she had been more thoroughly and more imaginatively punished for her reckless adventure than she could ever have imagined possible. But that too, she eventually realized, was a far-from-insignificant milestone in her increasingly complicated life.

CHAPTER V

Although no punishment had actually been agreed by the committee of her parents once Father Lemuel had sown the seeds of deep dissent, Sara still expected to be put under house arrest for at least a month after the hometree-climbing incident. She was somewhat surprised, therefore, to be invited to accompany Father Stephen and Mother Quilla on a junkie expedition to Old Manchester on the following Sunday. It wasn't until she mentioned the fact to Gennifer during Friday's school break that the reason became clear to her.

"It's not a treat," Gennifer told her. "It's what everybody's parents always do. If the whole lot of them can't stop arguing among themselves long enough to tell you off they delegate someone—or some two—to whisk you off somewhere quiet where the rest of them can't get in the way, so that they can give you a good talking to."

"They could do that in my room," Sara objected, even though what Gennifer had said had a suspicious ring of truth about it. "They often come in one at a time for little chats—except for Father Lemuel."

"It's not the same," Gennifer told her, shaking her head to emphasize the point. "Mine always do the most serious tellings off outside the house, on neutral ground. Davy said the same when I mentioned it to him, and Luke and Margareta confirmed it. I think it must be in the parents' instruction pack."

"Oh," Sara said. She considered the implications of this statement for a few moments before saying: "Well, at least I get a trip to Old Manchester out of it."

"I've never been there," Gennifer admitted. "Is it nice?"

"It's not *nice*," Sara said, smiling wryly at the thought. "But it is interesting. People come to the junk swaps from all over the country, and the ruins are...well, I'm not sure what they are, but they're not like Blackburn, or anything else around here. Father Gustave says they've been allowed to rot for far too long, and it's about time the reconstruction crews got busy, but Father Stephen says that the junkies need at least another fifty years to sort through the rubble if we're to save the Legacy of the Lost World."

"You're lucky to be near enough to go," Gennifer said. "We live in a town, but we're further away from civilization than you are."

"You can look at Old Manchester any time you want," Sara pointed out. You can set your bedroom window to look out on it. You can probably watch me at the junk swap if you want—I'll wave to a flying eye if I see one hovering. I wouldn't call it civilization, though. It's mostly just a mess. Anyway, Father Gustave says that civilization was what they had before the Crash—what caused the Crash. He says what we have now ought to have a new name."

Gennifer shrugged her shoulders, having no interest at all in Father Gustave's opinion on such abstruse matters, but she didn't have time to change the subject because break was over and their hoods had automatically tuned into the virtual classroom again—and not for anything as relaxing as a history lesson. Sara found elementary biochemistry extremely hard going, although she knew it had to be done. It was, after all, the stuff of life itself.

Gennifer turned out to be right about Father Stephen and Mother Quilla having been delegated to have a serious word with Sara about the climbing incident, but Sara was glad to discover that they were in no hurry to get on with it. Indeed, when they all climbed into the robocab clutching their lunchboxes and bags of junk, Father Stephen and Mother Quilla seemed even more enthusiastic than Sara to stare out of the window and pretend to be interested in the scenery. It wasn't until they were on the Old Roman Road that either of them took the opportunity to speak.

"This road is two thousand years old," Mother Quilla told her. "Well, not the road, but the route it follows. It's a lot straighter than many that were built after it."

"I know," Sara said. "I've been on it before."

"I only had six parents myself," Mother Quilla went on, without the least hint of a mental gear-change. "Father Stephen had four. Father Lemuel had to make do with two, just like the days before the Crash."

"Not exactly like," Father Stephen pointed out. "He wasn't biologically related to them—and his mother certainly didn't have to give birth to him."

"Details", said Mother Quilla, dismissively. "The point is, there were only two of them. Not four, or six... and certainly not eight. Two's a pair, eight's a committee. Have you ever seen a picture of a camel, Sara?"

"Yes," said Sara.

"Well, before they became extinct, people used to say that a camel was a horse designed by a committee. They didn't say how many people there were on the committee, but if it wasn't eight it might have been. The point I'm trying to make is that it's difficult enough for two people to agree, or compromise, it's more than twice as difficult for four, and more than twice as difficult as that for eight. There are people who think that eight people is too many to parent a child, and there's a real possibility that the Population Bureau will change policy if things don't seem to be going very well. Everyone's on trial, you see—the whole system as well as individual households. But if the new Internal Technologies do work as well as the manufacturers say, and the human lifespan really will extend to a thousand years as from today or tomorrow...well, you can do arithmetic. If anyone is ever to have the chance again of parenting more than one child—and if they don't, then how will they benefit from the practice?—they're going to have to form even bigger households than ours. So...."

"I only climbed the hometree," Sara pointed out.

"Yes, I know," said Mother Quilla. "It's not the climbing we're worried about—not any more. It's not being able to decide how to cope with it."

"I only wanted to see what I could see," Sara said, defensively. "I promise I won't do it again."

"It's not that, Sara," Father Stephen chipped in. "The point is, it won't be the last time that you do something that worries us—and in a way, it would be a great pity if it were. If you only ever did what we told you, you wouldn't be able to develop the independence you'll need to organize your own life when you go your own way. We just want you to understand what happened the other night. We feel that we let you down, you see, by not being able to form a united front and give you clear guidance. It couldn't be good for you to see us fall out like that."

"Oh," said Sara, unable to think of anything else to say.

"But it's probably inevitable," Mother Quilla said, taking up the thread again. "If eight people could agree about everything, we wouldn't need democracy. If eight people had ever been able to agree about anything really important, Old Manchester would never have been built, let alone ruined."

"It wasn't bombed," Sara pointed out, figuring that she needed to say something to demonstrate that she was following the argument. "The people had to move out to be nearer the facfarms when the petrol ran out. Not like London, or Jerusalem."

"It wasn't quite that simple," Father Stephen said, "but that doesn't matter. The point is that it's not unusual for eight people not to be able to agree. It's unusual when they do. Not that anyone thinks you should have carried on climbing the hometree when we told you to stop—except perhaps Lem, who'd always rather be in a minority than a majority if he possibly can, and would probably like you to grow up the same way."

"Which will be your decision," Mother Quilla put in. "Not now, but some day. What we're trying to say is that what happened on Wednesday night is normal, not something for you to worry about."

"I wasn't," Sara said, truthfully.

"Good," said Father Stephen, sitting back in his seat to signify that the conversation was over, for the moment—which was perhaps as well, because the robocab had drawn to a halt on the edge of St Anne's Square, where hundreds of junkies had set out their blankets full of petty treasures salvaged from anywhere and everywhere in the ruins of the pre-Crash world. From now on, Sara knew, Father Stephen would be in a world of his own: the world of the collector, the searcher for curious things whose value their present owners did not fully appreciate.

"You will stay with me, won't you?" Mother Quilla said, anxiously, as they got out of the cab. "You won't go off on your own?"

"No, I won't," Sara said, meekly, feeling that she owed Mother Quilla at least one promise, and maybe as much as a whole week of good behavior. In any case, the kind of crowd that was thronging around them now both was far too intimidating and far too vigilant for her to risk getting too far away from Mother Quilla's side. She knew only too well that if the impression got around that she were lost, there would be a great many more than eight people fussing around her furiously, until she was safely un-lost again.

She had to turn away, though, when a cloud of dust suddenly blew into her eyes. It had been whipped up by four bikes that had just roared past along the edge of the square. The riders—all male, she assumed, although it was impossible to tell—were decked out in all their finery, but Old Manchester wasn't the best place to show off peacock feathers and tiger-striped fur, because they always picked up a grayish patina of powdered concrete. The ancient city was being slowly ground down by the scourge of the westerly wind and the rainstorms it carried in from the Irish Sea. The dirt on the ground was thick and murky, having as much red brick and ground glass in it as concrete residues—but whenever a few sunny days allowed it to dry out it was the tiny particles of concrete dust that rose into the air like a miasma as the passage of pedestrians and vehicles disturbed its rest.

When she had rubbed her weeping eyes clear, Sara saw that a second cab in Blackburn's blue-and-silver livery had drawn up behind the one in which she had travelled. It was just disgorging its lone passenger.

Sara didn't expect for an instant that she would recognize the passenger, even though the cab must have kept close company with their own for almost the whole of its southward journey, but nor did she expect to be so astonished by the sight of him.

The man who got out of the other cab was almost as unfashionably tall as Father Stephen, and even thinner. Like Father Stephen, he had darkened the color of his smartsuit almost to black for outdoor wear, and there were hundreds of other people in the square whose dress was equally sober—but the resemblance ended at the neatly-shaped collar. Like Father Stephen and almost everyone else in the square, the newcomer had politely left his face exposed to public view, the smartsuit's overlay remaining quite transparent...but Sara had never seen a face like his before.

There seemed to be hardly any natural flesh lying upon the bones of the skull, and what there was bare hardly any resemblance to the soft contours of conventional adult appearance. It had a slight quasi-metallic sheen, which made it seem more like the skin of a lizard than a man...or like the polished plastic face of an android robot.

Although Father Lemuel was fifty-six years older than Father Stephen, and nearly a hundred years older than Mother Jolene, no one but a doctor or a master tailor could have read the difference in their features; whatever signs of aging Father Lemuel's flesh was prey to, his smartsuit cancelled them out. This man was different. This man's face was afflicted with all manner of stigmata, for which his smartsuit could not compensate, and which it could not conceal. Something terrible must have happened to him, Sara thought; it was as if he had been so badly burned in a fire that the even cleverest biotechnicians had been unable to repair the scars.

While Sara stared at him, he did not see her at first. He was looking in another direction. Then, as he began to turn his head to scan the crowd, he caught sight of her. He looked straight at her, and met her eyes. His expression changed, although it was not until some time afterwards that Sara, replaying the scene in her memory realized why. He had seen the horror on her face.

Oddly enough, Sara had not actually been conscious of feeling horror—she had interpreted her own reaction as surprise—but her face had shown it anyway. The man had been concerned, anxious to reassure her—but no sooner had he raised his arm slightly, and taken half a step in her direction, than he changed his mind. Abruptly, he turned away, thus hiding his face, and marched off into the crowded marketplace.

At the time it seemed rather rude; Sara did not realize for several minutes that he had done it for her sake, because he had thought it the simplest and easiest way to set her mind at rest.

"Who was that?" she whispered, as the man with the terrible face hurried away, clutching a rucksack twice the size and weight of Father Stephen's.

Mother Quilla followed the direction of her gaze easily enough.

"Nothing to worry about," Mother Quilla said. "It's only Frank Warburton. They call him the Dragon Man."

The image of the shop window in the Cloistered Facade of New Town Square surged out of Sara's memory with an uncanny brilliance, perfectly fresh, in spite of all the time that had elapsed since she had gone to see the fire fountain.

She had always assumed, without even knowing that she was making an assumption, that the Dragon Man had been called the Dragon Man because his shop had a dragon in the window. It had never occurred to her, and nothing anyone had ever said to her had carried the least suggestion of it, that the Dragon Man might be some kind of dragon himself.

"What's wrong with him?" Sara demanded.

"He's very old," Mother Quilla said, in what seemed to Sara to be a remarkably off-hand manner. "He was quite old—by the standards of his time, that is—when the first Internal Technologies came on to the market, and the preservative measures he took then weren't as effective as the ones that came later. He's not the oldest person in the world, by any means, but...well, you don't get many people his age turning up to junk swaps. Everybody in the north-west knows him. He's been around all our lives. I suppose it is a bit of a shock when you see him for the first time, though. There's nothing to be frightened of. Lem knows him from way back—Gustave too, I think. Well, *know* might be putting it a bit strongly. They were acquainted, maybe did some skintech business. He's into sublimate technology now. An example to us all—in the sense that it's good to know that you can still keep up with the times, even if you're two hundred and fifty years old."

"Two hundred and fifty?" Sara echoed, wondering why the number seemed so much larger than one hundred and fifty, which was Father Lemuel's age, give or take a few years. A quick calculation assured her that even two hundred and fifty wasn't old enough to remember the world before the Crash; it seemed just as remarkable, though, that Frank Warburton must have been born *during* the Crash, into a world in mid-collapse.

Frank Warburton, Sara realized, must not only have had to make do with two parents, or even one, but must actually have been born from his mother's own womb. In terms of human evolution, he was practically a dinosaur.

Or, at least, a Dragon Man: something rare and strange.

"He used to be a tattoo artist," Mother Quilla added, as if the thought had only just resurfaced in her mind. "He's probably here hunting for obsolete equipment. Electric needles, that sort of thing."

The way she pronounced the words told Sara that Mother Quilla hadn't the slightest idea what kind of equipment Frank Warburton had used in the long-gone days when he was a tattooist, even though she must have looked into the window of his shop a dozen or a hundred times.

Most of the people at the junk swap, Sara knew, would be trading ancient communications technology: primitive computers and mobile phones, sound systems and TVs. The currency of junk swap culture wasn't invisibly inscribed in smartcards and hologram-bubbles, but it consisted very largely of plastic wafers and discs— every obsolete means of data-storage that had ever been invented. Such wares were exchanged even by the minority of traders who had come to trade jewelry and toys, pottery and glassware, paintings and snowing globes, although none of them would ever have admitted that they were compromising the etiquette of barter by introducing any kind of "money". According to Mother Quilla, though, the Dragon Man was different. Even here, he was an anachronism, an outsider, an exotic specimen. He might not be the only collector of tattooing technology in England, or even in Lancashire, but could there possibly be another who had ever *used* that technology in his work...or in his art? Could there possibly be another who was so fully entitled to style himself a Preserver of the Legacy of the Lost World?

"Come on," said Mother Quilla, taking Sara's hand and drawing her gently away from the spot to which she had become rooted. "He's not that unusual. You must have seen people as old as him in virtual space."

It wasn't until Mother Quilla said it that Sara realized that she had not. She had certainly seen people from the old world—even the world before the Crash—but she had never seen them as she had just seen Frank Warburton, still carrying the damage inflicted on his flesh before the biotechnologists found ways to repair all wounds and set aside all signs of aging.

In virtual space, it was said, you could see everything. All the world was there, and all the world's accessible history, and imaginary worlds by the thousand as well...but that didn't mean that if you took the obvious paths through the Global Village you would be certain to see everything it contained. Some things went unheeded, even when they weren't hidden. That seemed, for a moment or two, to be an important revelation—but then Sara and Mother Quilla lost themselves in the crowd, and in the strange simmering excitement of the possibility of making discoveries.

CHAPTER VI

The first effect of Sara's unexpected encounter with the Dragon Man was to renew her interest in dragons—an inspiration that took hold of her while she was still in Old Manchester. She used up every scrap of her junk hoard to acquire three more figurines and an old flag depicting a red dragon on a green-and-white background.

When she returned home—after another long lecture from Father Stephen and Mother Quilla about the importance of family life—she dusted off her entire collection of models and repositioned them on her shelves. That evening, she went back to her desktop to discover what reference-texts that had previously seemed "too old" for her had to say about the subject, but rapidly tired of their tedious commentaries on the different kinds of dragon favored by various ancient cultures and the special significance of dragons in Chinese tradition. She was, however, drawn to a number of advertisements on one of the shopping channels, which offered "dragon experiences".

Sara already knew that there were numerous Fantasyworlds populated wholly or partly by dragons. She had looked out into several of them from her bedroom window. She had even entered one or two of them by means of her hood, which had placed her within the virtual worlds in question, allowing her to "ride" dragons as they flew through their virtual native skies. She had not found such experiences very satisfactory, because they had been far too obviously artificial. The "dragon experiences" that had now caught her eye boasted of a far greater degree of realism, whether one entered the imaginary worlds in question as a dragonrider or as a dragon. The ads promised that "you'll really believe that you're there"—and Sara couldn't help wondering whether they might be able to deliver.

The snag was that the "dragon experiences" in question needed not one but two supportive technologies. They required a cocoon capable of producing the sensations of touch and smell that a mere hood could not provide, and they required an injection of special nanobots whose purpose was to enhance such sensations from within.

Father Lemuel owned a state-of-the-art cocoon, which he was occasionally prepared to let Sara use for educational purposes. The nanobots were another matter entirely. So far as Sara knew, none of her parents was a habitual user of "entertainment IT," and it was not the kind of thing of which they usually approved. When the price of the bots was added to the Fantasyworld's access charge, the total was the kind of sum that could make Mother Maryelle roll her eyes in horror.

Unfortunately, Sara had no credit of her own with which to make direct purchases in the virtual world. When she became a teenager, an account would doubtless be set up for her, but there would be little point in asking for one now, even if she had not rendered herself open to an automatic refusal by climbing the hometree less than a week before. If she wanted to ride a dragon, or to be a dragon for a while, she would have to ask one or all her parents to fund the trip—and it was a lot to ask, even if she could convince them that the experience had real educational value.

There seemed little point in raising the matter at a house meeting, where it would only provide yet another issue about which her parents could argue. Father Lemuel was the only one who possessed a cocoon's whose inner lining could interact with her smartsuit cleverly enough to simulate the physical sensations required by the "dragon experience", and he also seemed to be the parent with the most money, so the sensible thing to do was to approach him privately. That wouldn't be easy, given that Father Lemuel spent so much of his time in the cocoon that he was rarely around to answer requests, but it was certainly possible. He was not a man who welcomed interruption, so it would be necessary to wait for the right moment, and to make the approach in the right way, but Sara was convinced that it could be done.

Fortunately, there seemed to be an opportunity to kill two birds with one stone. Sara was intrigued by dragons because she was intrigued by the Dragon Man, and—as more than one of her parents had pointed out to her—Father Lemuel knew the Dragon Man. At least, Father Lemuel had known the Dragon Man in some previous era of history, long before Father Lemuel had come together with her other parents to form the household in which she was now being brought up.

Sara knew that there was no need for Father Lemuel to emerge from his beloved cocoon to eat, excrete or exercise, but she also knew that he was not a man to ignore good medical advice. Even though people came to no particular harm if they remained in virtual space for weeks on end, popular opinion judged that it was healthier for the mind and body alike to spend time in the real world at regular intervals. Father Lemuel's excursions into reality were unpredictable, except for house meetings, and often occurred while Sara was at school, but she was confident that an opportunity for private conversation would present itself eventually, and she was prepared to be patient.

As it happened, patience wasn't required. Father Lemuel was as enthusiastic as all her other parents to follow in the footsteps of Father Stephen and Mother Quilla by taking her aside for a quiet chat. She didn't have to lie in wait for him—he came to her, while she was playing in the garden on Thursday evening, ostentatiously keeping a generous distance between herself and the hometree's wall. Mother Verena was weeding the vegetable patch and Father Aubrey was grooming his herbs, but they were both out of earshot from the swing on which Sara was sitting, rocking gently back and forth.

"Would you like a push?" Father Lemuel asked.

"No, that's all right," she said. "I can manage." She felt that she was now too old to require any assistance, or to take pleasure in such simple things.

"Did you enjoy yourself at the junk swap last Sunday?"

"I made some good swaps, but I'll need to find some new junk for the next one. Father Stephen did well, but he didn't get as excited as he sometimes does. Mother Quilla looked around, but she didn't swap very much."

"Quilla doesn't have quite the same attitude as Steve," Father Lemuel observed. "Her heart's not in it."

"She likes looking, though," Sara said. "She's not a *real* junkie—but I'm not sure that I am, either. I just like dragons. I saw the Dragon Man at the swap."

"Did you? How did he seem?"

"I don't know," Sara said, realizing that she didn't have any standard for comparison. "He was in a robocab that pulled up behind us. He saw us, but he went the other way and we didn't bump into one another again. I never saw anyone that old before. Will you look like that in another hundred years?"

"I doubt it," Father Lemuel said, soberly. "Nobody knows how long people with my kind of IT will be able to live, or exactly what will happen when it begins it fail, but I won't have to suffer the kind of ham-fisted repairs that he had to undergo when IT was in its infancy. He's more cyborg than I'll ever need to be."

Sara knew that everyone with Internal Technology—or even a smartsuit—was a cyborg of sorts, but that the term was only used for people who had considerable quantities of inorganic material integrated into their bodies.

"Can't they take the old repairs out and make new ones?" Sara asked.

"It's not that easy. It's safer to leave the old patches in place and keep adding new ones—if they tried to strip him back to the bare flesh, it would probably kill him. There aren't many of his kind left—and most of the others spend even more time in virtual space than I do. He's old in a way that people like us will probably never experience. People are picked off by accidents all the time, and there are still a few diseases that take their toll, but hardly anyone dies of *old age* any more. When Frank and his kindred are gone, we'll never see their like again."

Sara thought about that for a moment or two. "But he must have the same Internal Technology as you have," she said. "Unless you're much richer than he is. So why will he die of old age if you won't?"

"Money doesn't make that much difference," Father Lemuel told her. "And I suppose I might get to die of old age if I'm lucky—or do I mean unlucky? Anyway, Frank had already done most of his aging before he was fitted with the first primitive IT suites; he's been preserved, but not rejuvenated. He's lasted a lot longer than he or anyone else expected, given that so much damage had already been done, and bearing in mind that he's had a couple of bad accidents along the way. He's tough—nobody knows what he might yet be capable of, including him."

"He must remember the Crash," Sara said, to prompt further revelations. "That must be weird."

"After a fashion," Father Lemuel agreed. "As you get older, your distant memories are edited down, but they never disappear. You lose the sense of having been there, though—I don't suppose that Frank's memories of the Crash are very much different from the impressions other people obtain by studying history, or surrounding themselves with collections of pre-Crash junk."

"I always thought they called him the Dragon Man because of the dragon in his shop window," Sara said. "I didn't know he looked...different."

"He doesn't really have to," Father Lemuel said, pensively. "He could program his smartsuit to provide the illusion of a face much like anyone else's. I once asked him why he didn't, but all he said was that other people could program their smartsuits to look like him if they wanted to, and if they weren't prepared to take the trouble, why should he? It's not so surprising, when you consider that he's always made his living helping people to look different and distinctive. His smartsuit covers up his tattoos, though—and he still has those, from way back. He dresses very conservatively, but wearing a mask to complete the picture is a step too far, in his way of thinking. It's just the way he is—I don't think he's trying to make a point, parading himself as a walking *memento mori*."

"What's a *memento mori*?" Sara asked.

"A reminder that we're all mortal. Even now. Even if we can live forever—which we probably can't—we won't. Accident or disaster will get us in the end. We're not immortal with an eye-double-em, and probably not even emortal with an ee. We can always be killed—any day, any moment. That's why it's really not a good idea to go climbing without the proper equipment, Sara. You really should take precautions."

"That's not what you said at the house meeting," Sara reminded him.

"It's not a good thing for parents to become too paranoid, or to put too many restrictions in place," Father Lemuel said. "Where would it end? Forbidding you to leave the house...then your room...then your cocoon. You have to be free to calculate your own risks—and that's why you ought to calculate them in a sensible manner. You were foolish, Sara, and you didn't need to be. If you want to climb—and you should—you ought to make sure that you can't fall, or won't hurt yourself if you do. Frank Warburton's always been a climber, but he didn't get to two hundred and fifty, or however old he is, without taking precautions. You don't get to be a Dragon Man without being careful. Do you see what I'm getting at?"

Sara nodded.

"Some of the younger ones think I'm not taking this parenting business as seriously as I should," Father Lemuel observed. "They think I'm only doing it because it's one more thing to tick off on my career list. They think that I think that the fact that I put in more money than anyone else entitles me to take things easy and leave the real parenting work to them. Well, they're wrong. What I really think is that I'm a good deal older and wiser than they are, which might make me arrogant, but doesn't necessarily make the judgment incorrect. Most of them will be applying for another license at some time in the future—maybe more than one, if things go well for the world and space colonization actually gets off the ground—but the chances are that you're my one and only. I take it seriously, even if you think I'm just a boring old virtuality-addict."

"I don't," Sara said. Sensing an opportunity, she said; "Can I ask you a favor, Father Lemuel?"

"Why?" he asked. "Do you think I owe you one?"

"No," she said. "But I don't think you think you owe me a *no*, if you see what I mean."

"I think so," Father Lemuel admitted, with a wry smile.

"I want to take a special state-of-the-art dragon ride, but I don't have any credit...and my hood isn't...." She trailed off, not wanting to say "good enough" in case she sounded horribly ungrateful.

"Why do you want to do it?" Father Lemuel wanted to know.

Sara didn't know what sort of answer would be most acceptable, so it didn't seem to be a good time to be economical with her explanation. "I don't know," she said. "But ever since I went to see the fire fountain when I was six, and saw the dragon in Mr. Warburton's window, I've been...I mean, I know they were never real, like lions and camels, or even dinosaurs, but there's something...well, I don't suppose anyone ever went to Mr. Warburton and said *draw a camel on my back*, or even a *Tyrannosaurus rex*. But they did want dragons. Golden dragons with silver bellies. And it must have really hurt, to have needles pumping that much ink into their actual skin for hours on end. And he put one in his window, didn't he? Out of all the things he'd ever drilled into anyone's flesh, he chose to put the dragon in his window. So there must be something special about dragons...even if they're all fantasy, all pretend. I want to find out what it is. I've ridden one in my hood, but that's only pretend—I can float like that in school. I want to try the new Internal Technology that works in collaboration with a cocoon."

Father Lemuel frowned when she mentioned the IT, but he didn't react the way Father Gustave or Mother Maryelle would have, with automatic revulsion. Perhaps, Sara thought, he knew more about that sort of technology than she had assumed.

Father Lemuel wasn't in any hurry to give her an answer, but he obviously didn't want to keep her in suspense either. "It can probably be arranged, if it's safe," he said. "Let me look into it."

"Thank you," Sara said, warmly. She leapt off the swing and gave him a hug.

"But next time you take it into your head to do something silly," he said. "I think you owe me a few moments' thought and a *no*, don't you?"

"I'll try to remember," she promised, that being all she could actually promise with any real hope of keeping her word.

Apparently, it was enough.

CHAPTER VII

Father Lemuel filled the syringe very carefully, then pointed the needle upwards and squeezed the plunger to expel a small air-bubble. "This might hurt, you know," he said.

"No it won't," Sara assured him. "Just make sure you hit the right spot." She had already primed her smartsuit so that it had marked the most convenient entry-point to a vein and secreted a modest amount of local anesthetic.

Father Lemuel seemed more nervous than she was, but he got the job done. Then he gave a slight sigh. "You, er, might want to keep this just between the two of us," he said.

"I won't tell anyone," she promised—perhaps a little too readily.

"It's not that it needs to be kept secret," he assured her. "I could have told the others—it's just that they'd have wanted to call a special house meeting to discuss it, for hours on end, and I'd have had to listen to Gus and Maryelle banging on yet again about parental responsibility. Not that I have anything against parental responsibility. It's just the thought of wasting all that time going over the same old ground. I'm too old for all that."

So am I, Sara wanted to say—but she daren't voice the thought, even to Father Lemuel.

"Anyway," Father Lemuel went on, "what kind of an example would we be setting if we were responsible all the time? You need to know that there's such a thing as parental irresponsibility, even in the best-regulated of households. Are you all right?"

Sara felt slightly faint, but she knew that there was no need. The thought of all those nanobots sweeping through her bloodstream was a little disturbing, but she knew that she mustn't let her imagination get the better of her intelligence—not until she was safely enclosed in Father Lemuel's cocoon, when she would have to do her utmost to make sure that it did exactly that.

"Fine," she said, holding herself rigid.

Father Lemuel nodded. His cocoon was built into a corner of his sparsely-decorated room, so discreetly that an uninformed observer might have assumed that it was nothing more than a blister. A home-tree's walls were prone to the occasional disease that generated swellings, and such swellings nearly always afflicted corners, rounding them out as if to suggest that nature hated right-angles. Nature's swellings couldn't be slit down the middle the way Father Lemuel's cocoon could, however, and their interiors weren't equipped with artificial nerve-nets with nearly as many connections as a human brain.

Stepping through the slit into the soft interior always made Sara feel claustrophobic for a moment or two, but the sensation was preferable to climbing into a gel-tank, which she had to do every time her smartsuit needed modification. Once the slit had sealed itself again there was a moment when the world seemed to turn upside-down, as the pull of actual gravity was cushioned and replaced by the apparent gravity of a virtual world. Once the moment of transition was over, however, she was fully committed to the Fantasy-world, and it only took a minute or so for her to enter into the illusion wholeheartedly.

The dragon she had come to ride was at least sixty metres from head to tail, but that was partly because it had such a long tail and a long neck. Its body wasn't that much bigger than a robocab, if you didn't count the enormous wings and the huge clawed feet.

Sara had been half-expecting four legs as well as the wings, and a body more like a lion's than a chicken's, but this was a world she had never looked into through her bedroom window. She was delighted to see that the colors were exactly right; the dragon's scales were gold and silver—mostly gold on the back, but all pure silver on the belly—except for the hood behind its snaky head, which was intricately patterned in red and orange.

Sara had elected to ride the dragon rather than be the dragon, so she found herself perched—precariously, it seemed—on a little saddle at the base of the neck. She had stirrups for her feet, and improbably long reins to hold on to, but it wasn't easy to believe that any signal she sent to the creature's distant head would actually elicit a response.

It was even harder to believe it once the long neck and coiled around so that the dragon could look back at her with its huge snaky green eyes, flickering its tongue as if it thought she might make a tasty meal, small enough to take at a single gulp.

The dragon didn't say anything. She could have chosen a Fantasyworld in which dragons could and did talk, but that seemed like cheating. She wanted to fly with dragons that were just dragons, not pseudopeople in fancy costumes. The kind of dragon on which she was mounted was no more real than the other kind, of course, but it seemed somehow to be a little less contrived, a little less fake.

The dragon must have looked around to check that she was aboard and properly posed, because it only favored her with a single lofty glance of disdain before it turned back again to look down the precipitous slope of the mountain on whose pinnacle it was perched, and then up at the clear blue sky. Without further delay, it launched itself into the air.

Sara couldn't help breathing in sharply. This was where the temporary IT was supposed to kick in, to work from inside her body to empower the illusion. For a moment, her mind clung hard to the knowledge that this was only a manufactured dream, and that she was still in the hometree, in Father Lemuel's room—but then it relaxed. She wasn't taken over in any kind of scary way; she just relaxed into the experience. She allowed her disbelief to be suspended; she gave her consent to the fantasy.

And it did feel as if she were actually moving, with the airstream flowing past her increasing to a gale as the dragon picked up speed. When she looked down, it really did seem that the ground was far below, and that she really might fall if she leaned too far to one side or the other.

She knew that if she tried to do anything the Environmental Rules wouldn't permit, she really would "fall" out of the saddle. She wouldn't be hurt when she hit the "ground," and her own IT wouldn't allow the IT that Father Lemuel had injected to scare her to death on the way down, but she had asked for a more realistic adventure and that was what she was going to get. The thrill of fear that lanced through her was as sharp as the thrill of fear she'd felt when she realized that she really might fall out of the hometree's crown and hurt herself when she hit the ground. Compared with floating around the insipid and intangible corridors of her virtual school, flying through the thick, cool atmosphere of the Fantasyworld was vivid, penetrating and wildly exhilarating.

This, Sara thought, must be what Father Aubrey meant when he talked about "the speed trip."

The dragon didn't beat its wings; it merely spread them out, arching and tilting them to catch an updraft that surged up the side of the mountain. It settled into a glide almost immediately, and then began to turn in a lazy circle around the pinnacle, soaring higher on the ascending column of air.

Sara felt the rush of the wind in her hair and on her face, crisp and electric, but she felt quite stable in the saddle—if not quite *safe*, at least not unduly uncomfortable. She wasn't in any hurry to look down again, though. She looked up, into the bright blue sky, squinting against the sunlight, and she looked out at the jagged horizon, where range after range of snow-capped mountains extended as if forever.

She had read the program's supplementary literature carefully, even though she didn't quite understand everything that it contained. She wanted to savor the imaginary world to the full, so she had ploughed on determinedly, even through the technical jargon. If this world had been an actual planet rather than an image in the mind's eye of a machine, it would have been twice the size of Earth, with only a fifth of its surface covered by water—a multitude of lakes rather than a patchwork of oceans—and almost all the remainder crumpled like a rucked-up rug. Many of the peaks would have been worn down by erosion, their rough slopes gentled as if by millions of years of rainstorms and floods of melting snow. The program that was generating the world had grinding tectonic plates built into its binary bedrock, and new peaks would be thrusting up as the older ones were worn down.

Sara knew that the "world" had only existed for a hundred years or so, and that its actual evolution had been incredibly rapid—but within its world-soul it had an implicit existence that stretched billions of years into the past, and an assumption of evolution with all the patience necessary to bring dragons out of reptiles that had once been fish, which had once been wormlike invertebrates...and so on, all the way back to bacterial slime.

The world felt old. Sara was not quite sure whether that sensation was somehow being communicated to her by the nanobots, or whether it was something her own imagination was inventing—but either way, she was glad of it.

The dragon, on the other hand, did not seem old at all. For all its vast size and easy competence in the air, there was something youthful about it—or perhaps, Sara thought, she was only projecting her own youth upon it. And why not? She was here to enjoy herself, to be master of her own experience.

She drew slightly on the reins, trying to suggest to the dragon that they had circled the peak for long enough, and that it was time to undertake a more ambitious directional flight.

The dragon responded to her touch. It turned its back on the high-set sun, and straightened out its course, heading for a group of peaks so tall that they wore collars of cloud.

Now, Sara looked down into the valleys over which they passed, at forests and meadowlands, winding rivers and waterfalls, placid lakes. There was no sign of human habitation but there were other animals: great herds of shaggy herbivores making their way along their grazing trails.

If Sara had chosen to be a dragon she could have hunted as one, trying to pick off an infant herbivore, but dragons of this sort did not hunt with riders on their back. Sara wasn't sorry about that, nor did she resolve to return one day in a fashion that would let her use her simulated talons and fangs to kill, and her simulated mouth to swallow her prey. She only wanted to fly. She was not here to pretend that dragons really lived, but only that they flew. What the dragon symbolized was more important to her than its seeming scaliness and fleshiness, even though she had only the vaguest notion of what it did symbolize, for her or for anyone.

Oddly enough, although the dragon seemed to be flying half a kilometer above the ground—more as it passed over the deep-set valleys—she did not have as acute a sense of height as she had had when she had finally paused in the hometree's steeple-like crown. At first she thought that was because the new Internal Technology wasn't living up to its promises, but there was another factor involved.

In the hometree's crown she had felt as if she were still connected to the ground. The potential fall had been measurable against a solid vertical scale. Here, there was nothing between her and the ground but empty space, which had no sensible scale. The perceptible objects on the ground seemed very small, and she knew that their seeming smallness was a product of distance, but her kind of eyes could not make that distance meaningful—except when they flew close to a vertical slope, whose precipitousness would become abruptly obvious as her mind somehow changed gear. That never lasted for long, though; the dragon flew on and on, leaving all such tilted walls behind.

The special Internal Technology continued its efforts, but now that she had become accustomed to its effects she became increasingly aware of the differences between the sensations of "touch" it synthesized and the real thing. The texture of the Fantasyworld wasn't quite right. The saddle and harness she was holding, and the scaly skin she could reach out and stroke, certainly seemed to be *there*, but they lacked the subtleties of real-world solidity. The air caressing her face as she moved through it was more convincing, but Sara couldn't shake off the suspicion that it wouldn't have convinced Father Aubrey, or anyone else who knew what a real speed trip was like.

Even so, it was new. It was wonderful. It was worth the effort.

As the flight extended, Sara tried to imagine what she might look like from a viewpoint even higher in the sky, from which the flying dragon might appear to be skimming the surface below, like a fiery cross moving across an infinite field of grey and green, flattened out by perspective. Was that, she wondered, what one of Frank Warburton's tattooed dragons had looked like? Had they looked as if they were soaring over a body that was in fact a world?

No, she decided. The dragon in the shop window had been seen in profile, as if from an airship floating alongside it, as if the skin of the wearer were the sky and not the ground at all: an infinite absence rather than an immediate presence. Was that the impression his clients had been trying to achieve? Not magnification, but transformation?

She began to see other dragons now, some soaring around their domestic peaks, others perched on ledges close to nests where huge white eggs were resting. Were they near to hatching? There was no way to tell. Half a dozen smaller dragons fluttered upwards to fly alongside Sara's mount in brief formation, but none carried a rider, and none turned its great green eye to stare at her. She was not invisible, but she was not of interest. She was an alien visitor, but her presence was not so disruptive that she needed to be noticed, let alone feared.

There are thousands of Fantasy worlds like this one, Sara thought, *and there'll be millions more—more than anyone could ever explore, even in a lifetime like mine.*

CHAPTER VIII

Sara began to feel cold, and realized that her temporary IT was already preparing her for the end of her trip. In advance of being expelled, she would be slightly discomfited, so that she would not regret her return to her own reality and might even feel glad to be home and warm. The awareness that time was short made her concentrate harder, determined to make the most of the experience while it lasted. She stroked the dragon's scales with her left hand, feeling their peculiar quality, like adamantine silk. She looked from side to side at the huge wings, marveling at the elegance of their curvature, the awesome precision of their form. She looked back at the extending tail, undulating ever so slightly like an eel in shallow water, then forward at the stretching neck, the arched hood, the strangely tinted head.

She looked up into the blue vault of the imaginary heavens, leaning back to let the sun's radiance warm her swirling hair as if it were a halo. Then she looked down again at the valleys sweeping by, nourished by streams whose sources were snow-packed crevices, weeping as the sun's glow eased their excess without ever cutting through the tresses dangling from the icy summits. She looked at the clouds clustered about the highest peaks, hugging them tightly, stirred at their outer edges by breezes that were not nearly strong enough to dislodge their grip and send them tumbling across the sky.

For the first time in her life, Sara was struck by the sensation that this particular virtual world was actually *more real* than the actual one. She was old enough to know that the sensation was subjective, arising as much from the particular way she was *paying attention* as the cleverness of Father Lemuel's cocoon and the temporary IT, but did make her wonder why she never attended to her actual surroundings with as much intensity...and the answer, she realized, was that her actual surroundings were too familiar, that she had no choice but to take them for granted because that was the essence of her relationship with them. This was different; it had a dramatic quality that actuality could only produce in circumstances so extreme as to be terrifying. Only a virtual world could offer this special kind of vividness without anything but the most superficial, graceful and entertaining sense of threat. This was a purer kind of excitement than any available outside a cocoon.

Was that, she wondered, why people like Father Lemuel found themselves spending more and more time in virtual worlds, less and less in the real one. And what kind of virtual worlds did Father Lemuel live in, anyhow? Did he also ride dragons, or did he have better things to do?

It was, of course, impossible to ask. She was old enough now to know where the most significant taboos of adult life were set out, and to steer well clear of any violation.

Then the dragon began to descend again. It was, she had to suppose, a long way from home—much further than she was. Perhaps it would pick up another rider before it set off on the journey—or perhaps, for now, it had earned a rest.

"How was it?" Father Lemuel asked, when Sara emerged from the cocoon, stumbling as she readjusted to the drag of actual gravity.

"It was great," she said, trying hard to sound suitably enthusiastic, so that Father Lemuel would think that his money had been well-spent. Actually, she felt dazed and disconcerted, not yet ready to evaluate the experience accurately.

Father Lemuel nodded, understandingly. "But not so very much different from watching them through a picture window?" he suggested. "Not quite as gripping as climbing the hometree."

Sara looked up at her oldest father with a slight frown, but she didn't say anything. She wondered exactly how good he was at following the train of her thought.

"It *was* different," she assured him. "The new IT made it feel much more real."

"It's new to you," Father Lemuel observed, implying that it was far from new to him. "You'll get used to it." Obviously, her parents—one of them, at least—were not as innocent in the ways of "entertainment IT" as Sara had assumed.

"If you get used to it...," she began, before the suspicion that she might be asking a forbidden question made her pause.

Father Lemuel didn't seem to mind the personal nature of the implicit enquiry. "Why do I spend so much of my time in virtual worlds, if the experience is always inferior?" he finished for her.

"Some people argue that it ought not to be reckoned inferior just because it's different, but that isn't really the point. All VW addicts point out there's an awful lot you can do in the virtual world that you wouldn't attempt to do in the real world because it would be too dangerous—but that isn't really the point either. You already understand that the real purpose of synthesized experience is to open up opportunities that have no parallel in the real world. Dragonriding is only the first step. In a VW you can reduce yourself to the size of an insect or a bacterium, ride a spacecraft through the solar system and beyond, etcetera, etcetera...and you can visit hypothetical worlds very different from ours, where everything—including the laws of physics—has been altered, not according to anyone's constructive imagination but by manipulating the generative code. Do you understand what I mean by the generative code?"

"I think so," Sara said. "At bottom, everything in a machine is just a matter of switches being on or off. What you see in a window or a cocoon is a translation of a long string of ones and noughts."

"That's right. A lot of what you see on your desktop screen or through a window starts out as a picture, which is converted into generative code so that it can be reproduced—and the picture can then be made to move by means of an animating program. But you don't have to start with the picture. You can use code to generate imagery that no one has ever seen or imagined before: whole virtual universes, which can then be explored at the sensory level. Do you see what I mean?"

"And that's what you do all day—explore imaginary universes?"

"I used to, when I was working full-time. I wrote code to generate alien virtual environments from scratch, then checked them out, to see whether any of them were interesting. In those days, I was looking for commercial exploitability. It's how I made my money. Nowadays, it's more of a...well, I suppose Steve would call it a hobby, because that's what I'd call his junk-collecting. I'd probably call it a vocation, because that sounds much more serious. Not that I turn down the opportunity to earn more credit if I find something I can sell. Dragons were never my sort of thing, though. Somebody else collected the royalties on your little trip."

"I like dragons," Sara said, defensively.

"So I've noticed," Father Lemuel replied—although, so far as Sara knew, he had never actually come into her room to see the models on her shelves or look through her picture window. "It's okay to like dragons. The reason I started telling you all that was to explain why you can only go so far with dragons—or any other conventional invention of the imagination. Your own senses—touch as well as sight—have been shaped by millions of years of evolution to deal with the world you walk around in. Even virtual worlds that mimic the actual world as closely as possible can only reproduce an appearance, and your brain is never completely fooled by it. My cocoon is state-of-the-art, but state-of-the-art will never quite catch up with the texture of actuality, even with the aid of clever IT. You'll never get an adrenalin rush from climbing in a cocoon that's the same as the one you got from climbing the hometree, because your brain and your body will always know the difference. There are some kinds of experience where it makes very little difference—including school, playing games and chatting to your friends—but whenever an experience is really important to you, or whenever you want an experience to be really important, you'll be aware of that margin. That's why so-called VW addicts never really lose touch with reality. Reality is the only place you can get the *whole* sensation of touch."

Sara thought about that for a few moments before saying, "I really did enjoy it."

"I'm glad," Father Lemuel assured her. "It was new, closer to real experience than you've ever been in a Fantasyworld before—but next time, you'll be more conscious of the difference. And the time after that...well, I suppose I should let you find out on your own. It's that old parental responsibility coming through again, always making free with the warnings and the sermons. You have to learn from experience to get the full benefit from your senses—all you're born with is the potential. You'll notice that more and more as you get older. Maybe we should have created more opportunities for you already, but parental committees always tend to take things slowly. Maybe it was different in the old days—but maybe not. Maybe two parents did just as much worrying as eight, but couldn't share it out so easily."

"In the even older days long before the Crash," Sara said, spotting an opportunity to show off her learning, "most people lived in extended families, not nuclear ones. Our way is a return to normality, if you look at it that way."

"So they say," Father Lemuel agreed, although the tone of his voice proclaimed that he didn't believe it. "People will go a long way in search of arguments that support what they're doing. *It takes a village to raise a child* is a slogan that's been worked to death. Whatever we are, Sara, we're not a village that's been somehow collapsed into a single set of rooms and strewn around a fake tree like so many squirrels' nests, and we're certainly not a company of grandfathers and maiden aunts who've been drafted in to baby-sit— although I can see how it might seem that way to you."

"There are birds' nests in the branches," Sara told him. "Lots of them. And things with lots of legs. It's not just *our* hometree."

"No, it's not," Father Lemuel agreed. "And that's one of the reasons for making some houses look like trees, rather than hiding all their organic systems away in hollow walls, the way they do in town houses. It wasn't just our Crash—the birds and the bees nearly went the same way as the large mammals. Ecologically speaking, it pays to look after your insects—and your insect-eaters."

"Is that why you bought a hometree?" Sara asked.

"Not really," Father Lemuel admitted. "It was more to do with the kind of environment we wanted to provide for you—good for climbing, among other things, although I'm not sure that all of us had given our full consideration to that aspect of it. But as I said, people will go a long way in search of arguments that support what they're doing, and I never like to let one go to waste."

"If I had my own credit account," Sara dared to point out, al-though she knew that it might be taking a little too much advantage of Father Lemuel's good mood, "I wouldn't have to ask you to pay for educational trips to Fantasyworlds."

Father Lemuel laughed. "And the difference would be?" he asked, meaning that what she was really asking for was to be given the money now rather than later.

"I wouldn't have to ask so often," she pointed out.

"Well," said Father Lemuel, "that's one of the advantages of having eight parents. There's always someone around to ask, and you don't have to put too much pressure on any one of them. Except that it's always me you'd have to come to if you wanted to use a state-of-the-art cocoon. Which is why I was rather hoping that to-day's little trip would have been sufficiently disappointing to make you think that it might not be worth the trouble of coming back to me on a regular basis. You can put it to the house-meeting if you like, but I bet you can guess what we'll say, after we've discussed it for an hour or two."

Sara nodded, glumly. "All in good time," she said, glumly. "Maybe next year, or the year after that. I'm only ten, after all. There'll be plenty of time to make changes." She pronounced these sentences in a mocking way, to emphasize that she was not speaking on her own behalf."

"Just between the two of us," Father Lemuel said, "you might consider the possibility of sticking out for a firm timetable. It's a lot easier for people to make promises about tomorrow than to get immediate action, especially when there's a committee involved. But once something's on the record, the promise has to be kept. I know it's not as good as instant gratification, but the time passes—if you're clever you can lay down a whole trail of useful promises stretching way into the future. Of course, I'm only telling you this because it's educational. It'll get you into the habit of making plans, thinking constructively about your future, and all that sort of stuff."

Sara saw what Father Lemuel meant about people going a long way in search of arguments to support what they were doing, and knew that he would expect her to see it. When she grinned, he grinned back—and now they were both following one another's trains of thought.

"Thanks," she said, as she went to the door so that Father Lemuel could get back to his vocation. "I'll try it, and see how it goes.

She was so anxious to try it out, in fact, that she became quite insistent at the following Thursday's house-meeting, demanding that a date be set for the time when she could have a credit account of her own with sufficient funds in it to make serious purchases—not just trivia like new views from her picture window, but big things like major modifications to her smartsuit.

It was at that point that she realized that Father Lemuel's cunning scheme had its downside. By going so far in search of arguments to support what she wanted, she overstepped the mark. She conjured up anxieties that might never have crossed her parents' minds if she'd taken a softer line, and she'd done so within a matter of days of climbing the hometree—which already had stirred up a fine mess of anxieties that her parents had hoped to postpone for at least a little longer.

Once she had raised the possibility of her being able to order major modifications to her smartsuit without having to obtain specific parental permission that became a topic of discussion in its own right...as did several other, far more fanciful, suggestions that various Mothers and Fathers put forward as to how the kind of credit she was talking about might be spent. By the time the scarier items—mostly involving hallucinogenic drugs, entertainment IT, powergliders, or robocabs to venues so exotic she had never even heard of them—had been aired, her hopes of obtaining a promise to set up a substantial credit account on her next birthday had been utterly dashed. Indeed, her entire strategy was usurped by Father Gustave and Mother Maryelle, who contrived to rally a six-two majority behind the motion that Sara should not have a substantial credit account until her fourteenth birthday—which would given them a ready-made excuse to turn down any approach she might make in the meantime.

Father Lemuel voted against that motion, as did Mother Verena—but Sara wasn't entirely certain, as she watched her future plans being wrenched horribly out of shape, that Father Lemuel hadn't known all along that persuading committees to establish firm timetables could as easily work against one's interests as for them. He was, after all, a hundred and fifty years old—give or take a few—and the time he spent in virtual worlds hadn't yet caused him to forget how the real one worked.

CHAPTER IX

Sara knew, even at the time, that the decision taken at the house-meeting after the hometree-climbing incident hadn't been a total disaster. It did mean that she had to keep on making special applications for credit every time she wanted to buy something substantial, but she had established the principle that when she eventually did get her own credit account, there would be no conditions attached to it.

In particular, because it was the example that had started the big argument, she had it on the record that she could pay for major modifications to her smartsuit.

When she had first mentioned that possibility, rather carelessly, Sara had not had any specific modifications in mind. It had merely been an example of the kind of major purchase that she would eventually have to make, plucked out of the air with only the vaguest notion of what it might eventually imply. Even at the age of ten, though, she had been conscious of the fact that the time would one day come when that might be an important principle.

Sara had long grown used to looking upon her smartsuit as a mere necessity, and it had never occurred to her to object to the simplicity of the appearance it presented. Babies were often displayed to the public eye in all the colors of the rainbow, but ever since she had started school, where her image was required to maintain an appropriate sobriety, she had taken it for granted that the only choice to be made regarding the configuration of her second skin was the color she would wear from the neck downwards. The vast majority of young children—not just in England but all over the world—wore plain costume, with the possible exception of a single decorative motif or an occasional venture into elementary patterns. Even at weekends, when children were taken out to be shown off to the neighbors, a few zebra-strips or abstract swirls were considered perfectly adequate as decorations. The faces of shy children might be ingeniously masked, but their bodies were rarely allowed much latitude for eccentricity.

Sara had taken this for granted for so long that it came as something of a surprise when her lessons in elementary biotechnology finally caused her to realize, as she approached her fourteenth birthday, what ought to have been obvious for a long time: that young children's smartsuits were plain because they were, in certain key respects, technologically primitive. They were simply not equipped with the sorts of decorative opportunities of which adults sometimes took advantage. As children became teenagers, however, their smartsuits matured with them, and became considerably more hospitable to unusual decoration.

When she mentioned this realization to Gennifer during one of their on-camera chats, her friend inevitably pretended to have been aware of it for ages.

"It was different in the olden days," Gennifer informed her, loftily. "When people wore dead clothes they had whole wardrobes full of all kinds of bizarre bits, which they put on in all kinds of weird combinations. All they—the clothes, that is—had to do was *hang there*, so of course they came in all kinds of different fabrics and colors, with all kinds of buttons and beads and things attached. The people put them on every morning and took them off at night, and sometimes changed them around half a dozen times a day. We get an extra layer of skin as soon as we're born and it grows along with us for the next twenty or a hundred years...until something so new comes along that it's easier to strip us naked and start again than it is to do a what-d'you-call-it...."

"Somatic conversion," Sara put in, to show that no matter how smart her friend might pretend to be, she was the one had the more assured command of the jargon.

"Right," Gennifer agreed. "But what I mean is, *clothing* is only one of the things our smartsuits have to be, and not the most important one while we're growing up—at least the way our parents see it. There's hygiene and protection and all kinds of other stuff to make sure we and the smartsuits grow properly. Adults don't grow any more—unless they take up some kind of sport that needs longer legs or whatever—so their smartsuits don't have so much other stuff to do, and they have metabolic capacity to spare for fancy decoration. We're sort of half-way between, which is awkward. The opportunities are there, but we have to persuade our parents to let us take them. Have you seen Davy Bennett lately—out of school, I mean, on camera?"

"No," Sara admitted. She rarely talked to any of her other classmates desktop-to-desktop.

"Well, he's rigged his tag so that you can get a picture of his new outfit just by clicking. Spiders aren't my thing at all, and I can't imagine how he persuaded his parents to let him have them, but it'll give you some idea of what's possible."

"Davy has *spiders* on his smartsuit?" Sara said, incredulously.

"Shadowspiders. Just an example. Margareta says she's going to get a pair of doves, but she hasn't got permission yet. Are any of your mothers into birds? Mother Jenna's got bluebirds, and Mother Luisa's thinking about hummingbirds. I told her hummingbirds would be great, but she doesn't rate my opinion very highly, so maybe I should have said I hated them."

As it happened, none of Sara's mothers had yet been caught up by this particular wave of fashion, but she didn't want to give Gennifer an opportunity to imply that the members of her family were country bumpkins, so she dodged the question.

"Does that mean that your mothers have to eat a lot more?" she said. "I mean, if their shoulder-pads and head-dresses are going to fly around when they're out and about, they must soak up a lot of energy."

"They don't have to eat more unless they want to," Gennifer said, "but they do have to eat slightly different things. The birds are designed to pick up some of their own nourishment, but I think that's just an option—a gimmick."

"You mean they eat flies?"

"I suppose they could," Gennifer admitted. "Mother Jenna's bluebirds are vegetarians, though. Hummingbirds live on nectar from flowers, so Mother Luisa asked the last house-meeting about the possibility of re-planting the garden with special roses. Mother Leanne's all in favor, but Father Guy's against it because of his herbs."

"Our garden's big enough for flowers and herbs, and a lot more besides," Sara said, automatically taking the opportunity to score a point.

"So you're always telling me," Gennifer retorted. "I'll have to come visit one day, so that I can get lost in it. When you come to see me, we can go to the lake. You haven't got a lake, have you?"

"We're not very far from the river," Sara said, but she knew that it was a weak defense so she quickly changed tack. "Mother Verena wears flowers," she said. "Only little ones. It's more for the stem than the blooms, I think—it makes such a lovely pattern as it winds around her body. The flowers are like little blue stars. And she has leaves over her breasts. Mother Quilla and Mother Maryelle have shells, but Mother Jolene doesn't have anything decorative at all— just her smartsuit, although it has to be a bit thicker in places to provide extra support. In a way, though, that's more decorative. Mother Maryelle keeps looking at me and dropping hints about shells, but I don't want shells, certainly not in all the other places Mother Maryelle wears them. I'd rather have flowers, like Mother Verena. One way or another, I'm going to get whisked off to the tailor fairly soon."

Gennifer had her desktop camera zoomed in on her face, so Sara couldn't see anything below her neck, but when Gennifer glanced down critically Sara knew that the other girl must be making calculations of her own.

"I'd like birds myself," Gennifer said, "but they'd never let me wear birds *there*. They'd say it would be too provocative when they took off."

"Flowers," Sara said, firmly. "Better that than the kinds of feathers and furs that bikers wear. I think Father Aubrey has a couple of radical surskins hidden away, but he doesn't think that sort of thing fits in with being a parent."

"My Father Jacob's the same," Gennifer said. "And I bet Father Guy's got a skeleton or two hidden in his cupboard. But that won't make them any more sympathetic to any requests I make. Mother Jenna and Mother Luisa might take my side, because they'd be glad to think they'd inspired me, but I'd never get it through the house meeting. The moment I mentioned it, they'd all start pushing their own ideas. I'd probably end up in chain mail. Parents, eh?"

Sara contented herself with a sympathetic nod, but the conversation set off a train of thought in her own mind that was still running long all through the evening meal, when no less than five of her parents put in an appearance at the communal table to engage in hearty conversation about the latest ecological management statistics, the reclamation of Antarctica, the Gaean Lib anti-SAP demonstrations in the South Saharan Republic and the latest scheme cooked up by the Continental Engineers to speed up work on the sixth continent without re-raising the sea-level to the point at which New Shanghai and the Brahmaputran Confederacy disappeared beneath the waves again. Sara could never quite work out whether anyone except Father Gustave—who had done long service as a UN bureaucrat before taking time out for parenthood—was actually interested in such matters, or whether they thought that it was the sort of thing they ought to talk about at communal mealtimes for the benefit of her political education. Either way, she felt no particular compulsion to listen, even at the best of times, and now she had more pressing matters on her mind.

Until she'd complained about it to Gennifer, she hadn't really given much thought to the matter of an imminent trip to the tailor, partly because her early experiences of smartsuit checkups had seemed to her to be on a par with visits to the hospital to have her ever-growing population of nanobot assistants monitored, enhanced and reprogrammed—not the sort of thing that one wanted to dwell upon. Now that she was growing up, though, she had to adopt a different attitude, and see such expeditions as matters of opportunity rather than mere obligation.

She studied the costumes of her fellow diners more carefully than she had ever bothered to do before. Father Gustave and Father Stephen were wearing plain black, the mass of their smartsuits carefully bulked up on the shoulders and at other strategic points. Father Aubrey was slightly more daring, opting for a dark blue base with several extra decorations, including a silk-effect cummerbund and purple leg-stripes. Mother Jolene wore a lighter shade of blue, but her attire was as plain and conservative, in its way, as Father Gustave's. Only Mother Quilla seemed to be taking much trouble to individualize her appearance, although Sara didn't think that green— even ocean green—was the right backcloth to show off her seashell decorations to good effect.

Suddenly, the accidental detail of the promise that she'd extracted nearly four years earlier, that she could use her credit account to pay for major smartsuit modifications, clicked into clearer focus. She really did have an opportunity that she must be careful not to waste. If she didn't want her parents to decide whether—or how—her appearance ought to be adjusted to take account of her increasing maturity of form, then she ought to conceive a plan of her own, and be ready to put it into action. If she wanted flowers, then she ought to decide what kind of flowers she wanted, and if she wanted birds....

Even birds, she suddenly thought, were not the limit of potential ambition. If she were to decide that she wanted dragons....

So far as Sara knew, no fashion designer had yet got around to engineering solid dragons that could enjoy the same symbiotic relationship with a person's smartsuit as the synthetic bluebirds and hummingbirds that were all the rage in the more civilized parts of north-west England, but animal and mineral decorations were not the only ones available. The easiest—and perhaps the cheapest—way to augment the display capabilities of a relatively primitive smartsuit was to use sublimate technology: images made out of vaporous substances that had enough molecular memory to form cloudy shapes in two or three dimensions, bounded by "smoke-skins". When they lay flat on the surface of a smartsuit, they were "astral tattoos," but those which could take flight could reform themselves as phantom bats or owls—or even spiders, if she had taken the correct inference from Gennifer's comments on Davy Bennett's new costume.

The astral tattoos that Sara had actually seen were mostly black, formulated as the silhouettes of bats, birds or swimming fish—but images of that sort were almost exclusively worn by males. There was no reason at all why astral tattoos shouldn't be any color their wearer might desire, or any shape their wearer might desire. They might, for instance, be golden dragons—and Sara was certain that she knew where a man could be found who would be only too pleased to make that possibility an actuality: Frank Warburton, the Dragon Man.

For ten minutes or so, while she slowly savored her dessert—cassata siciliana, flavoured with three traditional fruits and three brand new products of ingenious genetic engineering—Sara solemnly considered the possibility of becoming host to a family of two-dimensional dragons, which would flow around her body, taking off from time to time to fly free like phantoms of eerie light, effortlessly upstaging any lumpen bluebirds or hummingbirds that happened to be around.

In the meantime, Father Gustave was earnestly explaining to Fathers Stephen and Aubrey and Mothers Quilla and Jolene why the as-yet-unbuilt supermetropolis of Amundsen City was the only appropriate home for the new United Nations Headquarters, with an enthusiasm that brought forth a mixture of laughter and astonishment.

"Surely, Gus," Father Stephen said, "even you can't actually want to live at the South Pole."

"It won't be cold inside," Father Gustave said, the reddening of his face uninhibited by the transparent surskin overlaying his native flesh.

"No, of course not," said Mother Jolene. "But think of the scenery! Even if they recreated penguins and polar bears from the gene banks...."

Sara was sure that Mother Jolene was joking, firstly because she had to know perfectly well that penguins and polar bears had lived a opposite ends of the Earth, and secondly because the Continental Engineers planned to reshape the glaciers in a massive crown-like rim around the reclaimed region where Amundsen City was supposed to be—but Father Gustave was blushing even more deeply as his frustration increased.

Whether the sight of that blush of annoyance that had anything to do with her own realization, Sara couldn't tell, but it came to her all of a sudden that it wouldn't do to be too original in her choice of sophisticated clothing. No matter what sort of promise was on the house record from four years before, she had to be careful not to overstep the mark, or the promise would simply be revoked. Politics, as Father Gustave was exceedingly fond of saying, was the art of the attainable.

Reluctantly, Sara set aside the idea of becoming a Dragon Girl, postponing further contemplation of that prospect until she was old enough to be a Dragon Lady. If she wanted to decorate her costume more elaborately now, she had to pick something that at least some of her parents would consider reasonable—which, given the constitution of the household, probably meant that birds were out of the question, let alone dragons.

Flowers, on the other hand....

While Father Gustave continued his pointless lecture on the virtues of Antarctica as a "Continent Without Nations" Sara thought about flowers, and their possibilities as bodywear.

"If you've had enough, Sara," Mother Jolene said, breaking in on her fierce concentration, "just put your spoon down and let the table get on with clearing itself. Don't play with your food."

"I'm eating it," Sara protested. "I'm just taking my time. I was listening. I don't see why Father Gustave shouldn't want to live at the South Pole when his work's done here. It'll be new, won't it? New's good, isn't it?"

No one seemed to suspect that this was the opening of a propaganda campaign, and it wasn't just Father Gustave who was grateful for her expression of opinion. All her parents liked to see her taking an interest in their topics of discussion, especially if they were only discussing them for the benefit of her education.

"Thank you, Sara," Father Gustave said, warmly. "It's good to have a sensible contribution to the conversation. "You really ought to set the child a better example, Jo."

"If I have to take your plans for the UN seriously," Mother Jolene retorted, "you ought to be a little more sympathetic to my interests."

"There's politics and politics," Father Gustave said, impatiently. "Gaean Lib nonsense isn't *practical* politics—it's romantic nonsense."

"That's a bit steep, Gus," Father Aubrey put in. "I suppose you think the sixth continent is romantic nonsense too."

"It is when people start calling it Atlantis re-risen," Mother Maryelle said.

"I didn't," Father Aubrey protested.

"And I didn't say that I was a Gaean Lib supporter," Mother Jolene put in. "What do you think of the Gaean Liberation Movement, Sara?"

"I think they're a necessary pressure group," Sara said, quoting an earlier remark of Mother Jolene's word for word, "but the same is true of the Continental Engineers—and in the meantime, the UN has to get on with the day-to-day running of the world."

No one seemed to notice that the second part of this careful judgment was borrowed from Father Aubrey, or the third from Father Gustave.

"That's very sensible," Father Gustave said. "Very mature, for your age."

"Well, I am nearly fourteen," Sara said. "I'll have my own credit account in a couple of weeks. I have to think of sensible and mature ways of using it."

While her parents were still congratulating themselves on the success of their educational discussion, Sara finished off the cassata in two gulps so that the table could get on with the next task in its schedule—which it did with such rapidity that she could almost have suspected it of impatience. The attention she had drawn to herself wasn't entirely complimentary, though. Mother Quilla was looking at her with a suspicious and slightly critical expression.

"Yes," Mother Quilla said, "you are growing up, aren't you?"

Sara could almost see the images of twin scallop shells forming in the mind behind Mother Quilla's contemplative gaze. Having made her impression, it was time to retreat.

"I've got homework to do," Sara announced, brightly. "Good night for later, in case I don't see some of you again."

So saying, she moved swiftly away to her room, barely pausing to wonder what the five of them would talk about over coffee, now that they no longer had to give such earnest consideration to her educational needs.

CHAPTER X

By the time the weekly house-meeting came around Sara had decided exactly what to ask for, and how to go about it. She didn't need to remind her eight parents that her fourteenth birthday was now imminent; they were almost as excited about it as she was. Nor did she have to remind them about the solemn promise that they had made four years earlier; the household's so-called artificial intelligence was slavishly dutiful about such matters of record.

There was the usual list of routine items to be sorted out. The hometree's roots had picked up yet another fungal infection, and because it was a new mutant the treatment might not be covered by the standard maintenance contract. The picture window in Father Stephen's room had developed a glitch and he thought that the replacement component ought to be bought out of the general household budget rather than coming out of his own pocket. *Et cetera, et cetera.* Eventually, though, the way was clear for Sara to make her bid.

"As soon as my credit account comes into operation," she announced, as though it were merely a matter of notifying them of something that needed no discussion, "I'll be going into Blackburn to have some modifications made to my smartsuit. I don't need anyone to accompany me, so it shouldn't interfere with anyone else's schedule."

"You can't go alone," Mother Verena said, immediately— picking up, as Sara had hoped she might, on the lesser of her two claims. It was the one she was prepared to surrender, if need be.

"She has to be allowed out some time," Father Aubrey obligingly chipped in.

"Yes," said Mother Verena, "but...."

"Hold on a minute," said Father Gustave, sending Sara's opening stratagem crashing to defeat. "What modifications? Your smart-suit doesn't need any modifications, Sara."

"Actually, I've been thinking about that myself, Gus," Mother Quilla said. "I've mentioned it to Maryelle, and Verena too. Sara's growing up. Whether she's allowed out on her own or not, it's only natural that she should begin thinking more carefully about her appearance."

"She's at school all day," Father Gustave said. "She has to follow the dress code."

"Her image has to follow the dress code," Mother Quilla pointed out, with slight exasperation at Father Gustave's willful stupidity. "Gus, even you must take note of what other children her age are wearing at weekends."

"We never see any other children her age in Blackburn," Father Gustave replied.

"Well, some of us go further afield than Blackburn," Mother Verena said. "Quilla's right—and so is Sara. This is something we need to talk about."

"Actually...," Sara began—but she wasn't allowed to get any further.

"From what I see down in ManLiv," Father Stephen put in, "teenage self-differentiation is more a boy thing than a girl thing...."

"*Teenage self-differentiation!*" said Father Gustave, scornfully. "Where on Earth did you pick up an expression like that?"

"You're a fine one to complain about jargon!" Father Stephen came back, testily. "It's what people are...."

Father Aubrey, who was in the chair, wasn't one to hesitate over using the claw-hammer. He brought it down with a sudden loud bang. "No childish arguments!" he said, abruptly. "Civilized discussion only, focused on the subject. Which is, if I read the direction of the discussion right, Sara cultivating a more grown-up appearance. Well, I for one think that if Sara wants to adopt a more adult image, we ought to encourage her."

"Why?" demanded Mother Jolene. "She'll have hundreds of years of adulthood. What's the rush? She doesn't have to be a fashion victim, now or ever. We ought to be helping her to resist that sort of pressure."

"At least for now," Father Stephen put in. "She can make up her own mind later."

Sara was strongly tempted to remind all her parents that they shouldn't be referring to her as "she" while she was actually present, but she knew from long experience that it would only waste more time. She sighed very audibly, but nobody noticed, so she leaned back in her chair while all eight parents continued to compete, pontificating about their various views on adult images and fashion victims. So far as she could tell, there wasn't the slightest possibility of a consensus emerging.

While the dispute continued its descent into chaos Sara took the trouble once again to look closely at the appearances her parents' smartsuits had been programmed to project. There was not the slightest variation in the five she'd previously inspected, and Father Lemuel's suit was even less elaborate than Father Gustave's, its thicker sections being even more sternly functional in the cause of decency. Mother Maryelle was obviously making more of an effort, but Mother Verena's flowers were the only example on view of anything that could pas for modern finery. The fact that Mother Verena worked outside the hometree, in ManLiv, had obviously given her a very different set of priorities; although everyone else in the household watched TV, it would have been a betrayal of their notion of parental responsibility to give any credence to the cults of celebrity that were driving the fashionability of smartsuit augmentations.

In the end, Father Aubrey had to reach for the claw-hammer again, in an ostentatiously purposeful manner, but the others were sufficiently alert to his intention to fall silent before he actually started banging. This gave Father Lemuel the opportunity to raise the big question.

"What kind of modifications did you have in mind, Sara?" he said, mildly.

"Well," Sara said, after taking a deep breath, "I've thought about it very carefully, and I've studied the examples set by all four of my mothers—and my four fathers too—so that I could see what each of you has done to make your smartsuits reflect your personalities. I've studied my classmates on camera, and the people on TV, to make sure I'd taken everything into account. After mature consideration, I've decided that what I like best is the kind of thing Mother Verena has—except that instead of a lot of little flowers, I'd like to start with just one, and see how that suits me before letting things get too elaborate."

All in all, she was satisfied with the speech. She particularly liked the reference to "mature consideration" and the final cautionary note about "letting things get too elaborate". They expressed the kind of sentiment that was sue to go down well—and she'd tried to make sure that no one could criticize her too harshly without seeming to criticize Mother Verena too.

Fortunately for Sara, Father Gustave was still in a stick-in-the-mud mood. When he said "Well, I don't approve of all this personal vegetation; it's almost as bad as phantom bats and ghostly scorpions—it looks absurd," he started a virtual stampede of disagreement, of which Mother Verena was merely a member.

Father Aubrey, having the chairperson's advantage, won the race. "I'm a conservative dresser myself, Gus," he said, unnecessarily, "but I never begrudged other people a little color. In our day, the technics weren't up to much more than that, so we never had the chance to play the kind of games that progress has opened up. We shouldn't be slaves to habit—it sets a bad example. We're supposed to be figuring out how to live for hundreds of years without getting bogged down in utter tedium. We need to be receptive to new ideas, new opportunities."

"That's fair," Father Stephen agreed, unexpectedly shifting his position. "There's such a thing as progress, Gus."

Father Gustave opened his mouth, probably to point out that Father Stephen was a man so deeply enmired in the past that his room was crammed from floor to ceiling with pre-Crash junk, but Mother Verena was keen to take up her own defense. "I'm not making any outrageous claims for my own taste, Gus," she said, "but I think wearing flowers makes a powerful statement about our relationship with the natural world. Two hundred years on, there's a danger that we might forget what our ancestors did to the world when they caused the worst ecocatastrophe since the Permian extinction. You must have some sympathy with that, or we wouldn't be living in a hometree. We thought that was the most appropriate place to bring up our child, and we were right—isn't it natural that a child brought up in a house whose organic systems are so flamboyantly manifest should want to accessorize that message in her own costume?"

That was a little too pretentious for Mother Quilla and Father Lemuel, whose simultaneous objections opened the floodgates. Everyone was suddenly trying to speak at once, and the claw-hammer had to restore order yet again. Patiently, the other seven took turns to respond to Mother Verena's argument with varying degrees of sympathy.

Sara put on a show of listening politely, carefully keeping her face straight. She didn't mind them arguing about the fine detail of Mother Verena's apologetic case. The more they bickered about matters of mere detail, she figured, the more likely it was that they'd forget to dispute the basic principle. She watched the arguments fly back and forth, as if they were moves in some ultra-complicated virtual game. There had been a time when the combative aspect of house-meetings had alarmed her, when she had wondered whether her parents might split up—as so many households seemed to do—but the anxiety had passed. Then, for a while, she had tried hard to be amused, in order to avoid being totally bored. Now, she sometimes found it interesting, if only as an insight into the vast differences of temperament, sensibility and opinion manifest in the little community that had come together purely for the purpose of raising her from birth to early adulthood.

Now, Sara was sensitive to the wonder of the fact that these eight strikingly contrasted people had formed an alliance, which consciously embodied a wide spectrum of jobs, ages and interests, in order that she should have a rich mixture of formative influences. In a way, the fact that they were always arguing was a great compliment to her importance in their lives—although, in another way, it just reflected the fact that they were all just a little to pig-headed for their own good.

In the end, a typically clumsy motion was finally put to the vote. It proposed that Sara should be allowed to take a robocab into Blackburn unescorted, in order to commission the family's tailor, Linda Chatrian, to augment her smartsuit with a discreet floral augmentation.

The result was a tie, four against four. Father Lemuel, Father Stephen, Mother Quilla and Mother Verena voted in favor, the others against. In theory, the casting vote was the prerogative of the chairperson—which was Father Aubrey, who had voted against—but Sara had a plan ready for this eventuality too.

"I think I ought to have a vote," she said, raising her voice just a little, so as to be clearly hard without sounding shrill. "I'll be fourteen by the time we meet again, and I think I ought to have a vote now."

Not unnaturally, her parents split four against four on the matter of whether to let Sara vote—and this time, Father Lemuel pointed out that it would be unjust to let Father Aubrey have a casting vote on that issue, because it was Father Aubrey's right to the casting vote that was in question.

Before Father Aubrey had time to point out that letting Sara decide would simply invert the problem by conceding the issue. Father Lemuel added: "The fact that we're taking a vote at all is a commitment to democracy, so why not extend that commitment to Sara?

It's her life we're talking about, and her smartsuit. Does anyone here really think that she's too stupid to be allowed a voice in her own affairs?"

Two years before, or even one, someone would have been sure to bring up the matter of her climbing the hometree as an example of Sara's irresponsibility, but time had healed that particular wound. It turned out that nobody wanted to take on Father Lemuel in an argument of this delicate kind.

"Well," said Father Lemuel, "that's settled. Everyone agreed?"

Everyone nodded, no one except Father Gustave with any manifest reluctance.

"Good," said Father Lemuel. "By the way, Sara, what kind of flower did you have in mind?" He smiled mischievously as he said it, and Sara smiled back, because they both knew that the opposition had missed that particular trick.

"Wait and see," Sara said, smugly. "You'll love it—but you'll have to wait and see."

And so it was that Sara called her own robocab the following Tuesday, charging it to her own account, and rode in solitary splendor into the centre of Blackburn, where she presented herself at the establishment of Linda Chatrian, Couturier.

CHAPTER XI

Sara had made an appointment in advance, and she was dead on time, so she was whisked through the reception area into the fitting-room without an instant's delay. Sara didn't doubt that Ms. Chatrian's patience had been severely tested by a bombardment of suggestions, pleas and warnings from her various parents, but the tailor smiled as politely as she would have smiled at any client of moderate means, and asked her what kind of augmentation she had in mind.

"I'd like a rose," Sara said. "One flower, to begin with, just *here.*"

"Would you like to look at a color chart?" Ms. Chatrian asked.

"That's all right," Sara said. "I know exactly what shade I want. How long will it take? I won't have to undress, will I?"

"No, of course not. You'll have to lie still for a while in the gel tank, but you've done that before. Roses are very popular, so I'll have no difficulty sorting out a cutting from stock, unless the color you have in mind is very unusual. I'll have to position it carefully, then program a growth-pattern into the resident nanobots...let's say two hours tank time, then a quick check-up, shower and home. The bud will take ten days or a fortnight to come fully into bloom. What about perfume?"

"Perfume?" Sara echoed. She realized immediately that although she'd spent a great deal of time at her bedroom window looking at florally-decorated smartsuits, she hadn't thought about scent at all—to study that, she'd have needed much better software, or the actual physical presence of the models.

"The flowers don't have to produce nectar," Ms. Chatrian explained, mistaking the reason for her hesitation. "If you don't want perfume, you don't have to have it."

"No, I want it," Sara said. "It's just that I haven't studied the options. If you have some kind of sample kit...."

"Of course," Ms. Chatrian said. "I'll get it for you. Would you like a little time alone to make your choice?"

"If that's no trouble," Sara said. "I don't want to hurry. It's important."

"Of course it is," said Ms. Chatrian. "It's no trouble at all."

Sara guessed that the tailor, as a matter of professional courtesy, would never dream of pointing out that the only people likely to benefit from the scent of Sara's rose in the near future were her eight parents, at least two of whom—and probably more—were sure to disapprove of whatever choice she made.

Ms. Chatrian ushered Sara into a tiny room that was little more than a cupboard with a wallscreen, with a hard round stool on which to sit. Patiently, the tailor showed her how to operate the equipment that would release scent into her nostrils, and then reabsorb the molecules to make way for the next sample. The position Sara had to take up in order that this could be done with maximum efficiency felt a trifle undignified, if not actually comical. Fortunately, Linda Chatrian had closed the door when she exited the room, to guarantee Sara's privacy.

"Take it easy," Sara murmured to herself, feeling that she was becoming slightly flustered by the unexpected sidetrack. "All the time in the world. Got to do this right." She knew that it wasn't just her parents who had to be shown that she could handle situations like this with calm authority; she needed to prove it to herself too. This was a big day, a day to set precedents.

As soon as she saw the catalogue list on the screen, though, the right choice leapt out at her with all the shock of a revelation. Even before she had sampled the scent, Sara knew that she had to have it. It was, she supposed, a bold decision—but this was a day to set precedents, and the rose itself was an advertisement of courage. Adding the right perfume was simply a matter of completing the design.

When she stepped out of the room again, Ms. Chatrian was waiting for her with an expression of exaggerated politeness that must have required centuries of practice to perfect. When Sara told the tailor exactly what color she required, and which scent she had chosen, Linda Chatrian merely nodded, as if she had expected Sara to make exactly that the decision.

The fitting eventually stretched to three and a half hours, and it cost a little more than Sara had anticipated—but she figured that her credit would just about stretch, provided that she kept her spending to a bare minimum until the end of August. Given that she hadn't yet grown accustomed to the ready availability of credit, that didn't seem too hard—and the sacrifice was surely justified.

She re-entered the house to find all eight of her parents lingering in the communal area. They weren't arguing. In fact, they were so busy pretending that they were there purely by chance, rather than because they were waiting anxiously to see what Sara had done to herself, that they seemed to be in closer harmony than they had achieved for at least seven years. That was good, because it meant that no one was in a bad mood that might be taken out on Sara's rose.

"The stem's wound around quite artfully," Mother Verena observed. "Linda's done a good job. The foliage will spread very nicely. More than adequate to protect your modesty." The last remark was accompanied by a sideways glance at Mother Quilla.

"I don't doubt it," Mother Quilla said, "but you'd have looked even lovelier—and better endowed—in a nice pair of shells."

Sara blushed at that, although there was no need.

"Considering the position of that bud," Father Gustave put in, "I think you'll be more comfortable if you don't grow too rapidly in that department."

Sara was conscious that her blush must be deepening even further. The bud was very small at present, but it was positioned above her breastbone, in what would one day be her cleavage.

"It's not going to get in the way when you sleep, is it?" asked Mother Jolene.

"Of course not," Mother Verena answered for her. "Even when the bloom's fully extended it'll fold up flat into the smartsuit if Sara smoothes it down with her hand and hold it in position for a few moments. You ought to do that when you take a shower as well as when you go to sleep, Sara, and you'll have to do it if you ever need to wear a spacesuit or a deep-diving surskin."

Sara didn't think there was any possibility of her taking an excursion into space or the remote depths of the sea in the near future, but she nodded anyway to show that she appreciated the flower's potential discretion.

"Well, I hope you like it," Father Aubrey said. "It'll be an expensive decision if you want something else in six months' time."

"It is detachable," Sara told him. "Ms. Chatrian told me that she can remove it and put it into storage any time—and that I could even do it myself if I followed the instructions very carefully. It can be stored warm for up to three years if the right provisions are made for its nutrition, or frozen down indefinitely."

Mother Maryelle leaned over her to inspect the tips of the petals that were peeping out of the bud. She sniffed ostentatiously, although Sara was fairly sure that there wouldn't be enough nectar in the flower to emit a perceptible scent for at least a week.

"Purple's a terrible color for a rose," Mother Maryelle opined. "At a distance, it'll look as if you're wearing a geranium."

"It's a bit dark," Mother Quilla said, placing her face beside Mother Maryelle's so that she too could inspect the tip of the bloom-to-be. "Imperial purple's all very well in broad daylight, but it won't show up well in less kindly light. You should have gone for a lighter shade. Mauve, perhaps."

"White, perhaps," Father Lemuel put in, a trifle mischievously. "All girls your age should wear white."

"Except that she was born on the wrong side of the Pennines," Father Stephen said, eager to show off his supposed expertise on the subject of pre-Crash culture, although there couldn't have been anyone present who didn't know that Lancashire's emblem was a red rose and Yorkshire's a white one. "She could hardly wear red, though, considering the kind of signals that would have given out—not to mention the fact that it would look as if she'd been shot in the chest. Or maybe in the back, given that it would look more like an exit-wound."

"It's not going to have thorns, is it?" Father Aubrey asked. "You're spiky enough without, these days." The last remark was sufficiently unfair to win a frown even from Mother Maryelle.

"Thorns," Sara informed Father Aubrey, with all due dignity, "are optional."

For a while, it almost seemed as if no one was going to ask about the as-yet-unmanifest perfume, but Mother Maryelle wasn't going to let her ostentatious sniff go to waste. "I do hope it's not going to be too strongly scented when it opens," she said. "It might be your rose, but the hometree's everyone's personal space."

"You'll hardly notice it," Sara promised. "It's called colibri."

Mother Maryelle—who knew no foreign languages—simply looked puzzled, but Father Gustave, always enthusiastic to occupy the intellectual high ground, tipped her off. "Colibri's French for hummingbird," he said. "Very nice, I'm sure."

Mother Jolene was the only one who picked up the full implication of that revelation. "Does that mean that the flower will attract hummingbirds, when it's mature enough to start producing nectar?" she asked.

Sara admitted that it would.

"There aren't any hummingbirds in England," said Father Stephen, frowning slightly because he already knew that he must be missing something.

"Oh yes there are," said Mother Quilla. "More and more with every day that passes."

"Those silly things that some women have started wearing on their shoulders and around their waists?" Father Gustave said. "But they're not real hummingbirds—just fancy costume jewelry."

"They might not be products of natural evolution," Mother Quilla told him, "But they're certainly real—a lot more solid than these astral tattoo things that all the young men are wearing, although some of them can apparently fly free too. Costume hummingbirds have real feathers, real wings and real beaks...and they have real appetites too. They drink nectar from flowers—and it seems that the flowers don't have to grow in gardens. What possessed you, child? There aren't any hummingbirds here. Or are you trying to drop heavy hints about *our* dress sense?"

"Of course not," Sara assured her. "I just thought it would be nice, when I go into town, or down to Old Manchester for junk swaps. Any hummingbirds around, far from their gardens at home, will be grateful that I'm around...and if there aren't any hummingbirds, the scent will just dissipate on the wind. It *is* discreet, just as Mother Maryelle wanted."

Father Lemuel stifled a laugh.

"Well," said Mother Jolene, with a sigh, "I suppose it's a nice thought, in its way. The flower is sterile, I hope—the hummingbirds might be carrying pollen on their beaks from real roses."

"Of course it is," Sara assured her.

"As a matter of interest," Father Stephen inquired, "do they make a nectar that attracts suicidal nightingales?"

Father Gustave was the only one who laughed out loud at that, and he didn't take the trouble to explain why. He and Father Stephen had always had a penchant for keeping their private jokes under wraps.

Although four of her parents had voted against the rose, all eight of them seemed sympathetically interested in its progress during the following two weeks—but theirs weren't the reactions in which Sara was most keenly interested. She did what Davy Bennett had done, adding an icon to her name-tag so that anyone in the school who cared to click on it could see a picture of her new costume—and she made sure that the rumor got around as quickly as possible, although that was hardly difficult.

As she had hoped, but had not dared to expect, the rose harvested a very satisfying crop of envious admiration. The only augmentation that offered any competition at all within her own age-group was Davy's spider web, but his shadowspiders weren't allowed to detach themselves from his person—not, at any rate, within the walls of his ManLiv town house.

In the mixed-age groups of the games sessions and hobby clubs the rose didn't seem exceptional at all, because practically everyone in the years ahead of Sara had some sort of additional decoration by now, but it felt good to be a pioneer among her peers, even if everyone else caught up by Christmas. Indeed, Sara congratulated herself on having set a standard which others would now have to strive to meet.

"I'm having birds myself," Gennifer reminded everyone, during morning break, although Sara knew that Gennifer had yet to negotiate this through her own house-meeting.

"I'm having snakes," Luke Grey boasted. "Not shadowsnakes—solid ones."

"With real poison?" Davy asked, oozing incredulity.

"As much real poison as your spiders," was the inevitable retort, "and my snakes will be in color"—after which Luke and Davy drifted off to conduct an earnest discussion on whether or not spiders were supposed to be poisonous, or whether they were just as creepy without, and, if so, whether the same arguments were applicable to snakes.

Even Sara's class teacher, Ms. Mapledean, was suitably impressed when Sara invited her to click on her new icon after class resumed. "What a pity we won't get the benefit of the scent," she said. "On the other hand, I suppose it might be inconvenient to have all the hummingbirds lurking behind the scenes in the year eleven classroom fighting amongst themselves to insert themselves behind the scenes this of one."

Sara laughed dutifully at the weak joke.

"My snakes will eat hummingbirds," Luke said, missing the point. "And they won't need to smell them first—so the rest of you had better watch out for your accessories."

"I think we ought to be able to duplicate our real suits in our school images," Davy Bennett said.

"I don't," Leilah Nazir retorted. "I wouldn't mind Sara's rose, but there's no way I'm going to sit in a classroom with your spiders."

"You'd better be careful with that sort of talk," Ms. Mapledean advised, "or the school governors will start talking about a real uniform again. It keeps coming up, you know. Allowing students to wear different colors was a hard-won compromise—if you start pressing for the right to display your animal, vegetable and mineral baubles, you might get the opposite result."

"You can't make us all wear identical smartsuits," Leilah said, incredulously.

"They don't have to, you idiot," said Julian Sillings. "All they have to do is to make us reprogram our virtual images."

"But it would be terrible if our images all looked exactly the same," Gennifer complained. "We wouldn't be ourselves any more. We'd be pretending to be all alike. That's pre-Crash thinking."

That's silly too," Julian observed. "Our *faces* wouldn't have to be identical, would they, Ms. Mapledean?"

"Why do you say that it's *pre-Crash thinking*?" Ms. Mapledean demanded, eager to set the discussion on a genuinely educational path.

As soon as normality was restored, Sara settled back into her customary half-attentive state of mind. She already knew why uniformity was one of many ideas that had been irredeemably tainted by the Crash, and knew that it had much more to do with armies than schools. Personally, she thought that all her teachers went on far too much about the sins of the pre-Crash world, given that everything was utterly different now and that no one had the slightest desire to make the same mistakes again.

When the lunch break rolled around and she could spend some time one-to-one with Gennifer, Sara voiced this opinion, and Gennifer readily agreed.

"It's a pity about the nectar, though," Gennifer said. "Living in the wilds, the way you do, you're not going to attract many hummingbirds."

"I don't live in the wilds," Sara said. "Blackburn's a bigger town than Keswick—I just don't happen to live in the middle of it.

Mercifully, Gennifer didn't want to argue about that. "It was a good decision anyway," she said, generously. "I can't wait till the flower opens out—it'll really suit you. And it will attract hummingbirds, every time you go out. The only thing half as sexy as wearing the very best living jewelry is wearing flowers that attract the very best living jewelry. You're going to have more blossoms than one, I hope?"

"In time," Sara told her.

"Of course," Gennifer agreed, oozing pretended sophistication, "You'll have to mind your diet now, though. You're eating for two. Drinking, anyway—the roots will be tapping your veins, even if the leaves and stem can...what's the word?"

"Photosynthesize," Sara supplied, automatically.

Father Gustave had told her, almost with nostalgia, that when he had been Sara's age almost everyone had worn their smartsuits black because the suits themselves had been able to fix solar energy just as plants did—or, to be strictly accurate, just as SAP-systems did. SAP—which stood for Solid Artificial Photosynthesis—was even more efficient than Mother Nature's chlorophyll, because it absorbed all the light falling upon it instead of reflecting the green part of the spectrum back again. Father Gustave had been trying to imply that he and Father Stephen had good reasons for continuing to wear black, but Sara knew that modern smartsuits were too complicated to get all the energy they needed from sunlight, even in places where it rained a lot less often than it did in Blackburn. Even so, she knew that he did have a point. All smartsuits might be parasitic nowadays, but some were undoubtedly more parasitic than others, and the energy supporting her suit's further decoration would have to come out of her own metabolism.

Gennifer had used the phrase "eating for two" in order to echo another taboo of pre-Crash times, before artificial wombs had replaced the inefficient ones provided by Mother Nature, but even its literal meaning was not completely free from macabre undertones. The larger Sara's new implant grew—whether it put out more flowers or not—the more support it would need. Quantity wouldn't be a problem, but Linda Chatrian had warned her that she would have to make sure that the rose's additional dietary requirements were met if she wanted the flower to reach it full potential. The kinds of whole-diet manna with which the hometree's pantry was abundantly stocked had no special supplements for the manufacture of nectar or the pigments in rose petals, and the supposed luxuries in which her various parents routinely indulged were similarly underequipped. Sara was already paying more attention to the fine details of her diet than she ever had before.

"You're right, of course," she said, to Gennifer. "It's a big responsibility. But I'm ready for it. So are you. Your parents will understand that—they're a lot more fashion-conscious than mine."

THE DRAGON MAN, BY BRIAN STABLEFORD

"I hope so," Gennifer said, with a sigh. "I certainly hope so."

CHAPTER XII

It would have been nice, Sara thought, once her own birthday party was over, if there had been a particular day on which her flower was due to open out—a sort of birthday of its own, which could be celebrated by a suitable invented ritual. Her party had been as much of a success as could be expected, given that all eight of her parents had been involved from start to finish. The virtual world in which it had been held had not only been selected but custom-designed by Father Lemuel, so it had been carefully tailored to her interests, but the great majority of the participants—parents as well as guests—had been using their hoods, so it had been little more than a light show. There had been dragons—not to mention roses and hummingbirds—but there had not been any real intensity, nor any particular sense of companionship...and nothing special, in any intimately personal sense.

Unfortunately, the flower's expansion was too gradual to permit the identification of any unique moment of achievement. Thirteen days elapsed between the bud's first tentative opening and the full display of the flower, which still had to acquire its final conformation and polish—a process which took a further week.

Sara's eagerness to see the process through to its conclusion sometimes seemed almost unbearable. She was so obviously impatient that her edginess brought forth a veritable flood of thorn jokes, not just from Father Aubrey but from everyone else—except Father Lemuel, who had not been seen in the communal area of the house since graciously accepting everyone's thanks for arranging her birthday extravaganza. He attended two house-meetings on camera, even though he would only have had to walk thirty metres to come to the table in person, because he didn't want to unhook himself from some special neural interface he was busy testing.

Father Aubrey joked about Father Lemuel too, saying that he was nowadays too far adrift in the virtual multiverse to notice anything that happened in mere meatspace even if it were "handed to him on a plate". The point of the remark was that Father Lemuel hadn't seen a plate for a month or more, having been perfectly content to take all his nourishment intravenously within his cocoon. Sara didn't think the joke was very funny, because she often worried about whether Father Lemuel was really safe when he spent such long periods in his cocoon. Father Aubrey and Father Stephen both liked telling scary stories about people who died in their cocoons and weren't discovered for months—although Mother Quilla assured her that it couldn't happen nowadays, because even the artificial idiots that passed for artificial intelligences in hometrees far less sophisticated than theirs could react immediately and effectively to medical emergencies.

When Sara repeated this assurance back to Father Aubrey and Father Stephen while they were in the garden one evening, they retaliated by telling her that modern smartsuits had now become so smart that they could walk around for days or weeks after the people inside them were dead. Father Stephen told her that such zombies were regularly to be found in attendance at junk swaps, offering the moon on a stick to any charlatan who claimed to have a ready-made elixir of life. That was far too tall a story to obtain an instant's credence from Sara, but she couldn't help wondering whether it might come true one day in the not-too-distant future.

"Of course," Father Aubrey added, changing tack yet again when he saw that Sara wasn't fooled, "Lem's smartsuit is specially programmed to make sure nothing happens to his body while, as he quaintly insists on putting it, *his spirit is on the Other Side*, so...."

"He doesn't say any such thing," Sara said, cutting the new horror story off before it had a chance to become silly. "Father Lemuel's a real explorer. And he *makes* new virtual universes, too. You shouldn't say nasty things about him when he put so much money into the hometree."

Father Aubrey had the grace to laugh at that, and apologize, but Father Stephen frowned as he jabbed his trowel into the soil of the herb garden. Weeding was a task he always performed with a slight attitude of disgust, even when Father Aubrey—who was the herb garden's designer and principal apologist—was actually present. "Lem's got no right to go on to you about how much he put into the hometree," Father Stephen said. "We all put in our fair share. You never see Lem out here, getting his hands and knees dirty. We all

91

worked for a living until we took time out, and I still go into the ManLiv factory three days a week. We can't all do our jobs in Virtual Space—someone has to tend to the sharp end. No matter how smart your software is, you need machines to carry them out, and machines need engineers. *Real* engineers."

"We all get our hands dirty now and again, Steve," Aubrey said, soothingly. "Even if some of us are a bit reluctant to kneel down in the dirt. You need to be more careful with that trowel—you'll injure the roots of the rosemary. Sara wasn't accusing us of not doing our share, were you, Sara?"

"No," Sara said. "I just didn't like you being nasty about Father Lemuel."

"You don't have to take his side because you think he got you the vote in house meetings, and your precious rose," Father Stephen said. "Everyone who casts a vote does it with the best of intentions."

"Sara knows that, Steve," Father Aubrey told him, speaking even more gently. "And she knows who takes her to junk meets, in spite of having to work three days a week, and who used to give her good stuff from his collection so that she could swap it for dragons."

That did the trick. Father Stephen got up from his kneeling position and drew himself up to his full height—as he always did when he wanted to seem impressive, although Sara suspected that he'd merely been seized by a sudden awareness that his carping was only making him seem ungracious. "And that's why you should take us seriously," he said, "when we give you solemn warnings about zombies in smartsuits and cocoons that turn into coffins. *We* know about things like that."

"And thanks to you," Sara told them, grinning to show that she wasn't serious, "so do I."

And so the time went by, until the rose had not only opened all the way but had acquired its final veneer and begun to secrete its nectar. It was then that Sara realized that there *would* be a particular moment to mark its maturity after all: the moment when the rose was visited by its first nectar-seeking hummingbird.

Not unexpectedly, though, that didn't happen right away, even though the perfume was a little less discreet than she had promised her parents. The nectar's scent was certainly subtle, but it gradually built up in the dining room until it became distinctly noticeable.

"If this goes on," Mother Jolene observed, when everyone except Father Lemuel was gathered for dinner one Wednesday evening, "we'll have whole flocks of hummingbirds zeroing in on us from every point of the compass every time we open a window—and it is July, going on August.

"I don't notice it myself," Sara said, blushing slightly. "I've got used to it. But the scent dissipates very quickly in the open air—I've had my bedroom window open for three nights running, but not a single hummingbird's picked up the scent as yet."

Father Aubrey seemed to be amused by this admission, but it seemed that he couldn't think of a joke in time to slip one in. Father Gustave took a more practical approach to the issue. "It's just that no one has bothered to program the air-filters to take the perfume molecules out," he said. "If you can't stand it, Jo, you're very welcome to pop down to the cellar and retune the system yourself. I could try if you want me to, but Lem's the expert"

"There's no need," Mother Quilla put in. "The wallskin will adapt automatically—just give it a couple more days. You didn't complain fifteen years ago when we had the nursery decked out with wallflowers, Jo."

"I thought they were gillyflowers," Mother Maryelle put in.

"Technically...," Father Stephen began—but no one wanted a pedantic sermon on the precise etymological implications of the words "wallflower" and "gillyflower". Mother Verena was quick to say: "Have you seen any hummingbirds yet, Sara?"

Sara admitted, by means of a shrug, that in spite of opening her window every evening to provide a means of getting in, she had not.

"It'll be different when we next go to Blackburn," Mother Verena assured her. "There'll be plenty of people out and about showing off their living jewelry."

"Your rose will probably be mobbed," Father Aubrey suggested. "You'll be fighting off hummingbirds with both hands. Mind you don't damage any, though—we can't afford a lawsuit, even if Maryelle offers her services for free."

Mother Maryelle—who worked as an investigating magistrate, weighing up the cases put together by opposing sides in legal disputes—did not dignify this comment with a reply, so Sara felt free to do likewise. The conversation soon reverted back to the usual political issues, including profoundly unexciting commentaries from all and sundry on ongoing UN debates regarding the redevelopment of Antarctica, plans for the redevelopment of the Furness Tip, proposals for changing the livery of Blackburn's robocab fleet and the chances of Yorkshire beating Lancashire in the annual cricket match at New Trafford.

When Sara went back to her room after dinner she opened her window immediately, and then called Gennifer for a chat.

Inevitably, "Any hummingbirds yet?" were Gennifer's first words too—but Sara had her camera set to close-up, so there was no point in shrugging her shoulders again.

"Not yet," she said. "If we lived closer to the cityplex it would be different, but hummingbirds are thin on the ground in these parts."

"They never touch the ground," Gennifer pointed out, pedantically, "so whatever they're thin on, it isn't the ground."

"I'm not going to give up," Sara said. "If I leave my window open long enough, one's bound to pick up the scent eventually, even if the perfume has to drift as far as the outskirts of Blackburn. Sometimes, I wish my parents hadn't decided that a rural environment was best for child-rearing."

"You'll have to visit me here before the summer's over," Gennifer said. "By August the twelfth we'll both by fourteen, and it's high time we met in the flesh. Isn't it too late now, though? I mean, evening's when people want their living jewelry about their person. You might do better to open the window tomorrow morning, if it weren't for school. Maybe you'd do better to wait for the weekend, or the holiday—we'll be out of school for a whole month after the end of next week."

Sara didn't want to wait for the weekend, although she could see the logic in what Gennifer had said about the evening not being the best time to expect other people's finest feathered frippery to be flying free. She had said that she wasn't going to give up, and she had meant it. She decided that instead of closing the window when she went to bed she would leave it open all night. The most likely time of all for costume jewelry to be left to its own devices, she figured, was when its owners had gone to sleep. Unlike roses, hummingbirds couldn't just flatten themselves out; they would presumably have to be detached. How far might they fly when they were? They must have some sort of programming to restrict their range, but how far would they be allowed to roam? On the other hand, anyone who had a flock of hummingbirds had make her own provision for their nourishment, If so, there must be more than one garden in Blackburn where colibri-scented roses were blooming in their hundreds—in which case, far-flying birds might find more abundant supplies of nectar much closer to home than her bedroom....

A further flaw in her plan, Sara realized soon enough, was that if she were actually going to witness any crucial moment that did arrive, she would have to stay awake herself—which might not be easy. She had to remind herself that she didn't have to stay awake all night, but only long enough for the first questing hummingbird to appear. Nor did she have to stay fully awake, so long as she dozed lightly enough to become alert at the first flutter of tiny wings.

It was with this thought uppermost in her mind that she finally laid her head on her pillow—having refrained from dimming her nightlight, on the grounds that it would be no use hearing the flutter of tiny wings if she couldn't see them beating

CHAPTER XIII

It was the repeated momentary eclipse of the nightlight that eventually brought Sara out of a light doze with a sudden start. She hadn't heard wings because the flyers that were zooming around her room weren't making any noise.

As she emerged from sleep Sara's heart leapt with anticipatory joy—but it only took two fleeting moments for her delight to turn to confusion, and then to disappointment.

The flyers weren't birds at all. They weren't even solid. They were like dark clouds seen in a speeded-up videotape, moving with impossible rapidity—except that real clouds were chaotic, never holding the merest semblance of shape for more than a moment. These clouds were very precisely shaped, sculpted into the image of living beings by some mysterious internal force.

They were, she realized, bats—not *real* bats, but shadowbats. They were astral tattoos.

She had seen astral tattoos on people's costumes at least a hundred times by now. From the relative safety of the virtual schoolyard, she had clicked on Davy Bennett's tag in order to watch his ghostly spiders quit their spectral webs to flow across the floor of his bedroom-which was, it appeared, the only place save for the contours of his body where they were currently allowed to flow. Flowing across flat surfaces was what all shadows did, though, and the astral tattoos she'd seen—including Davy's spiders—hadn't seemed particularly remarkable even in the absence of real objects to cast the shadows in question.

The shadowbats flying about her room, on the other hand, were doing something that no shadow ever had, or could: moving through space with effortless ease, maintaining distinct three-dimensional forms in spite of the fact that they had no solidity.

THE DRAGON MAN, BY BRIAN STABLEFORD

Father Lemuel had once shown her the interior of a gas-giant world—not a real one, but a serious simulation put together by experimental xenobiologists—which was populated by thousands of different kinds of vaporous life-forms. Many of them had been far more spectacular than these invaders, which were mere mimics of solid creatures that still existed in spite of the Crash, no bigger than her adolescent hand—but the gas-giant's inhabitants had been phantoms in a virtual world, where phantoms belonged. The shadowbats were in her own world, in her own bedroom, where phantoms had no possible right to be. That made them bizarre and disturbing.

Sara knew that there must be hundreds, if not thousands, of young men in Blackburn, Preston and ManLiv whose smartsuits had been adapted to support shadowbats. The augmentation was slightly less expensive, and far less troublesome, than the one she had undertaken. People who routinely wore black to go abroad in the world, like Father Stephen, could wear such augmentations unobtrusively even to their places of work. There was, in consequence, nothing very surprising about the fact that she should eventually see shadowbats in flight, nor about the shadowbats themselves. Even so, they seemed bizarre—and their presence in her bedroom, where they had no right to be, was disturbing.

Sara wondered, briefly, whether the bats might belong to Father Stephen, who could have been concealing them about his black-clad person for months, but she quickly rejected the idea as absurd. It did not even seem conceivable that they might belong to Father Gustave. In fact, the only one of her parents Sara could imagine as a potential shadowbat-wearer was the youngest of them all, Mother Jolene—but Mother Jolene was so adamant about her immunity to fashion trends that she surely would not contemplate such a step until everyone else had passed on to a new fad. Anyway, it was absurd to imagine that any of her parents could have been keeping a secret flock of shadowbats, so the shadowbats could not possibly belong in the hometree.

They must, therefore, have come from further afield—which meant that they must have flown a long way...unless there was someone lurking in the darkness just beyond the garden hedge.

That thought made Sara sit up on the bed, looking anxiously at the open window—but she stayed where she was, and watched the shadowbats.

There were six of them. They were as graceful in flight as only semi-substantial creatures could be. They spiraled and soared, dived and looped.

As soon as Sara sat up on the bed, the rose began to open out. It had obediently flattened itself out when she had smoothed it with her hand, so that its petals would not be crushed as she turned over on the bed, but it responded automatically to her change of attitude.

Immediately, the flock of shadowbats moved towards her—or rather, towards the flower. Now, when they dived, they descended one by one upon Sara's not-quite-flattened rose, banking as they slid past its burgeoning surface, like swallows skimming the surface of a wind-rippled lake.

For a moment or two, Sara assumed that they were only playing, perhaps attracted by the unusual color of the flower. She quickly realized, though, that they really were taking turns, moving past the flower in strict rotation, as if they were sharing its effluence.

Unlike hummingbirds, the shadowbats could not hover; nor did they possess beaks which they could intrude into the centre of the flower so that they might drink directly from the nectar-glands at the base of the style. In any case, because they were vaporous themselves, they had no need for vulgar liquid nourishment...but Sara realized that this did not mean that they needed no nourishment at all, nor that they were unequipped to take it from the air.

It took Sara several minutes to become convinced of the fact, but in the end she could not resist the conclusion that the sublimate organisms really were taking in the volatilized scent of her rose's nectar, absorbing the perfume into their cloudy bodies a few molecules at a time. They had neither mouths nor noses, so they were not drinking or breathing it, but they were certainly mopping it up—her own nose told her that much.

It was only a short step from that conviction to another, which was that the shadowbats' aerial frolics were becoming more hectic by the moment. It seemed to Sara that they were not merely absorbing the intangible perfume of her purple rose, but also becoming intoxicated by it, as if it were a drug.

For a few moments Sara remained absolutely still in her sitting position, marveling at the unexpectedness of it all—but then a sense of violation began to build.

A rose perfumed by colibri nectar should not be attracting shadowbats. None of the scents in the catalogue shown to her by her family's ultra-respectable tailor were designed to attract shadowbats, nor had she ever seen such an advertisement on TV, even on the more exotic shopping channels. The shadowbats that had invaded her room might not be guilty of theft, given that the scent exuded by her flower could not be reckoned to be *hers* once it was released into the air, but they certainly seemed to her to be guilty of some strange as-yet-unnamed perversion.

So far as Sara knew, shadowbats were designed to draw their nourishment parasitically from the bodies of their hosts. Unlike ornamental birds and bees, they were not intended to seek out "food" elsewhere. Their flight was not supposed to be purposeful. But Sara was old enough to know that "so far as she knew," at the ripe old age of fourteen, was not very far. The world was still full of mysteries that her schooling, her parents and her TV-viewing had not yet contrived to illuminate. What she did not know about sublimate technology would easily fill a catalogue, if not a whole virtual world.

Her train of thought suddenly turned back on itself, returning to her supposition that shadowbats were nourished "from the bodies of their hosts"—or, more likely, host in the singular, if she were only concerned with the particular flock of night-visitors turning somersaults around her nightlight.

These were not just any shadowbats; they belonged to someone. In fact, they belonged to the kind of person who was likely to wear, at least some of the time, an elaborate network of quasi-Gothic astral tattoos. Someone like Davy Bennett, but probably older. One of the year elevens or twelves in webschool...or someone even older than that. Not necessarily male, but very probably. Someone who lived nearby, at least insofar as "near" could be defined by the flight of an insubstantial bat...or someone who was nearby now, wherever he might live....

This time, Sara did jump to the floor and move away from the bed, scattering the shadowbats as she did so. Not one of them touched her, nor even came close enough to her face to let her feel the faint wind of their passage. She went to her east-facing window and looked out into the sultry late-July night.

The stars were bright, only a few of them hidden by wisps of cirrus cloud. The moon was in its third quarter, a crisp white crescent. Away to her left, the muted streetlights of Blackburn—which were designed to minimize light pollution, but could not prevent some leakage of their emissions—imparted an eerie glow to the northern horizon. The familiar sky seemed almost neighborly in spite of being out of reach—but the ground was cloaked in black, and might have hidden a hundred silent watchers who could see her silhouette quite clearly, while remaining utterly invisible themselves. So far as she could tell, the whole surrounding countryside might have been swarming with people...or shadowspiders, shadowscorpions and shadowdragons.

Her parents had always assured her that the hometree was absolutely secure. Nothing could get past the perimeter undetected, they had told her. The hometree's resident artificial intelligence was clever enough to identify any intruder, and frustrate any malevolent plan that any intruder might have. Burglary was one of the many crimes that had been put away with the sins of the pre-Crash world.

Even so, there were people who liked to wander about by night, especially in the season when the normally dreary north-west of England retained a calm echo of Greenhouse Crisis subtropicality. There might easily be someone out there beyond the property's boundary... someone whose presence might be entirely innocent, quite devoid of any criminal intent, but which could still be reckoned disturbing.

Sara reached out into the night to pull the window shut—and as soon as she did so the shadowbats reacted. Vaporous entities had very little scope for awareness, let alone intelligence, but whatever organizing power controlled their bat-like shape was sensitive to the fact that the window was their only means of escape.

They flew past her in tight formation, and were gone. The night dissolved them, almost as though it were absorbing them into its own vast void. It was as if they were themselves no more than a perfume to be obliterated even as they were sensed.

For a few seconds, Sara remained frozen in mid-motion, unable to complete her intention. Then she was free again, and she drew the window closed, without undue violence. The intense darkness she looked into now was not the darkness outside but the darkness of another world, which the pane was programmed to display. It was not one of her favorite dragonworlds but a forestworld...a lush tropical jungle, of a kind where hummingbirds might live wild, if the natural species had not been exterminated by the collateral damage of the ecocatastrophic Crash. No stars were visible through her window now, because the rainforest canopy was too dense to let even one shine through...but Sara had never been sure whether that meant that the virtual world in question was bounded by the opaque canopy, or whether the stars were somehow "there" even if they could never be seen.

As her Internal Technology calmed any unnecessary fear that the strange visitation had excited, Sara began to feel very tired indeed. She moved back to her bed, and lay down upon it. She curled herself up slightly as she smoothed her rose with her hand, until its petals merged with the gentle contours of her flesh.

It was only a dream, she told herself, silently, although she knew perfectly well that it had not been a dream at all. *It was all shadows and illusions*, she added—but she was old enough to know that she lived in a world where shadows and illusions had to be taken seriously, because they were usually meaningful products of ingenious design.

CHAPTER XIV

In spite of the deep dent in her credit inflicted by the rose, Sara decided to take a robocab into town on the following Saturday morning in order to consult Linda Chatrian about the shadowbats. A few eyebrows were raised when she told the five parents lingering in the dining room that it was expected, but they conscientiously respected the rights they had recently conceded by asking no further questions when she told them that she was "only going into town". After much thought, she had decided against telling any of her parents about the strange visitation. She was afraid that one of the four who had supported her initial request might decide to switch sides and begin a campaign to have the rose removed and put in storage until the mystery was sorted out.

The moment she had been waiting for arrived almost as soon as she stepped out of the cab. The street was crowded with strollers and shoppers, at least some of whom had come out to parade their finery. Two hummingbirds appeared as if by magic, and began to engage in an intricate competitive dance to determine which of them would have the privilege of taking the first sip from Sara's rose.

Sara paused, knowing that she ought to be savoring the moment and storing it away as a precious memory, but she was suddenly overtaken by a flood of self-consciousness. Although the pedestrian traffic hadn't actually come to a standstill, it had visibly slowed. People were not only looking at her but actually modifying their pace, or even coming to a halt, in order to watch her.

Sara had been aware for a long time that heads would turn whenever she came into town, and that her presence was always being noticed by passers-by. On the whole, though, the people who noticed her did so discreetly. It simply wasn't done for strangers to look too long and hard at a child, let alone speak to one. Sara always looked at other children herself, and almost always recognized any who were within two or three years of her own age, but the etiquette involved in two groups of parents coming together to negotiate any contact more elaborate than a casual nod and a friendly smile was complicated, and there never seemed to be any pressing need to make contact in real space when contact in virtual space was so easy and relaxed.

This was different. For one thing, she was unescorted. She was also sporting a decoration manifestly designed to be noticed and admired—not to mention the two hummingbirds dancing in the air before her.

For the first time in her life, Sara became acutely conscious of the difference between merely being noticed and being the centre of attention.

She didn't wait to find out when and how the hummingbirds would settle their dispute. She bolted for the door of Linda Chatrian's shop. It wasn't until she heard it slide shut behind her that she paused to regret the fact that she must have looked like a silly coward to thirty, forty or even fifty pairs of interested eyes.

She had to pull herself together as she approached the desktop in reception, glad that it was only manned by a screen-based AI. *Start again*, she instructed herself, firmly. *You have to get used to being out and about without half a dozen parents forming a protective wall between you and the world.*

Fortunately, Ms. Chatrian wasn't busy. Sara didn't have to sit in reception for long—which was perhaps as well, given that Sara had always found the tailor's reception area rather uncomfortable. It was so very clean and orderly by comparison with the communal rooms in the hometree that she was always anxious about the possibility of leaving accidental smudges on the glossy furniture, or misting the polished surfaces of the desk and occasional table by breathing out too vigorously.

"It's coming along nicely," the tailor observed, warily, when Sara was admitted to her presence. "Any hummingbirds come fluttering round it yet?"

"Two, when I got out of the cab," Sara admitted. "There might be a problem."

"What problem?" Ms. Chatrian asked, through slightly-pursed lips.

"I left my window open the other night," Sara explained, "but no hummingbirds flew in. I got shadowbats instead."

"Really?" said the tailor. "They're quite pretty when they're in flight, aren't they? I've had a few requests for sublimate accessories, but they're not quite my style. Sublimation technology is progressing by leaps and bounds, so I suppose we'll all get used to it soon enough, but detachable shadows...I was talking about them to your Father Stephen only the other week, and he called them 'airy-fairies from Cloudcuckooland'. It's a joke, you see...."

"I know," Sara said, patiently. "Father Aubrey told it to me before he told it to Father Stephen, and Father Gustave explained it. The shadowbats were attracted by the scent of the rose. They were soaking it up from the air—getting drunk on it."

"I'm sure you're mistaken, Sara," Ms. Chatrian said, in her most imperious adults-know-best voice.

"I'm sure I'm not," Sara countered, feeling that she had been cowardly enough for one day.

Linda Chatrian was too worldly wise to be so easily wrong-footed. "What did your parents say about it?" she asked.

"I haven't told them," Sara said, flatly. "I thought it was a matter between you and me."

"Me?" the tailor said, disingenuously. "I don't see that it concerns me. I supplied exactly what you asked for. Colibri is designed to attract hummingbirds...but I suppose that whatever smells sweet to hummingbirds is bound to smell sweet to other things as well. Shaped sublimates may be simple entities by comparison with creatures of flesh and blood, but they need some kind of sensory apparatus to guide themselves around, and smell is the obvious one to use. It's not entirely surprising that they might be attracted by a strange scent."

"They were absorbing the perfume," Sara said, doggedly, although she knew that she had no proof of it but her own conviction. "It had an effect in them."

Ms. Chatrian made as if to shrug her shoulders, but thought better of it. Her slim shoulders, conspicuously unadorned by hummingbirds or any other modern frippery, were perfectly designed to illustrate contempt—but that wasn't an attitude Ms. Chatrian wanted to display to a customer whose family were regulars. "I'm very sorry, Sara," the tailor said, "but I don't think there's anything I can do anything about that. If there's a complaint to be made—and if what you say is true, I certainly agree that there might be—then it ought to be addressed to the manufacturers of the shadowbats. I'm sure they'll be interested to know that their nice new technology has a good old-fashioned glitch."

Sara observed that Ms. Chatrian's voice was slightly smug as well as casual. As a tailor who hadn't yet involved herself with the new technics, Linda Chatrian was not in the least displeased by the thought that they might have thrown up an unfortunate side-effect—but she obviously didn't want to get involved if she could avoid it.

Sara thought about insisting that Ms. Chatrian ought to help her find out what had happened, but decided that the tailor was right. If she had a complaint to make, she really ought to take it up with the people who had made the intoxication-prone shadowbats. If, on the other hand, she were merely curious—Sara hadn't quite made up her mind about that—the supplier would be more likely than a tailor to be able to give her further information.

"If the shadowbats were local," Sara said, determined to get some profit from the meeting, "Who's most likely to have fitted them?"

"It's not really my field," Ms. Chatrian replied, cautiously. "I wouldn't like to make accusations based on guesswork. There's a matter of professional ethics, you see...but I can check the local section of the web-directory for you, if you like."

Sara made no reply, but the tailor turned to the desktop anyway, tapping away at the keypad with a single slim finger, as if she were too refined to type with all ten fingers. After a few seconds she said: "There are three sublimate technologists in Blackburn, five if you include Preston. If you widen the search as far as ManLiv...."

"That's all right," Sara said. "Perhaps the Dragon Man will know. His shop's just around the corner."

Ms. Chatrian turned back to look at her then, obviously relieved to have the matter taken out of her hands. "Yes, of course," she said. "Bats would be his sort of thing, wouldn't they? He's quite cutting-edge, in spite of the fact that his window-display's all needles and blades, and he certainly attracts clients interested in...the macabre. Your Father Lemuel would probably patronize his establishment rather than mine, if he cared about appearances at all."

Sara knew an opportunity to score a point when she saw one, so she said: "Well, perhaps I'll take a look at his catalogues myself."

Unfortunately, Linda Chatrian wasn't in the least intimidated. "I'm sure he'll be only too pleased to help you," was all she said in reply, without the slightest twitch of her professional smile.

Sara made the most dignified exit she could contrive, and squared her shoulders as she stepped back into the street, ready to defy the crowd no matter how intense its stares became. While she was standing there, preparing to take her first step in the direction of the New Town Square, the two waiting hummingbirds resumed their intricate dance—but now they were quickly joined by two more.

"Oh, this is ridiculous," Sara murmured, just loud enough to be heard by the nearest passers-by. She marched off, nursing a growing sense of resentment at the fact that the long-anticipated moment hadn't worked out at all as she's hoped and expected.

The four hummingbirds followed her, fluttering around her head as if in panic. It was obvious that that none of them was ever going to be able to find time and space enough to hover before her rose and sip its lovely nectar, unless she intervened in their contest. For ten or fifteen paces she refused to do that, intending to hurry as quickly as she could to the door of the Dragon Man's shop—but then she remembered the pang of regret that had afflicted her when she heard Linda Chatrian's door close behind her.

What a fool the watching crowds would think her, to have fitted a rose with colibri perfume, and then to think that questing hummingbirds were a nuisance to be avoided.

She slowed down as she crossed the square, until she finally came to a halt beside the fire fountain. There were parents with little children ringed around it, posed in attitudes of dutiful awe—but the parents were already glancing surreptitiously in Sara's direction, and some few of the children had already tired of the rain of shimmering sparks.

When she first reached out with her hands Sara felt very awkward, and was afraid of seeming as awkward as she felt, but the hummingbirds' tiny brains were programmed to expect and respect human guidance. She had no difficulty at all in waving three of the birds away, so that they paused in patient expectation while the fourth took up a position at the mouth of her rose, and politely extended its beak. Then, as easily as if she were a practiced expert—although the skill was all to the birds' credit—she let the others descend, one by one, to take their turns.

Because she was in a place where everyone routinely stopped to stand and stare, there seemed nothing particularly unusual in the fact that she was surrounded by curious gazes.

Why shouldn't they watch? she said to herself, silently. *Why shouldn't they enjoy it, given that it's there to be enjoyed?*

A few cool sparks from the over-energetic fire-fountain drifted sideways in the breeze, falling upon and around her, extinguished as soon as they made contact with the flesh of her smartsuit. She couldn't tell whether the adults watching her were admiring her flower or secretly condemning her as a pathetic show-off who ought to be old enough by now to be less avid for adult attention, but she was confident that the rapt attention of the little children was honest. After all, she had once been a child herself

Ten minutes later, the hummingbirds were sated and Sara had more than enough courage in reserve to step up to the Dragon Man's shadowed door. She passed through it as soon as it opened to her touch.

CHAPTER XV

Unlike Ms. Chatrian, the sublimate technologist manned his own reception desk—which was situated in a room as different from Ms. Chatrian's tastefully sterile, user-friendly, pastel-shaded antechamber as anyone could imagine.

The Dragon Man's shop was dingy and dusty, and the walls were covered in dead pictures rather than window-screens. So far as Sara could tell, the only screen in the room was the one on the desk on which the proprietor was currently resting the absurdly boot-like soles of his smartsuit. The lamp on his desk was placed so that it illuminated the chair on which clients might sit; his own face was in shadow.

Sara knew that the Dragon Man looked older than anyone else she had ever seen in the flesh, but, even though she was standing much closer to him now than she had been when they had exchanged a single speculative glance four years before, she couldn't she him clearly enough to make out the details of his remarkable face. What she could see clearly, though, was that there wasn't anything remotely like the image of a dragon on his delicately-patterned smartsuit. His nickname suddenly seemed woefully ill-fitting. There didn't seem to be as much of him within his extra skin as there was of most people, and Sara was slightly embarrassed to be reminded of Father Stephen's gleeful recitation of the urban legend about people who wore suits so smart that they kept right on going when their wearers died, until nothing was left of the individual inside but a mere skeleton.

"Hello, Miss Lindley," the Dragon Man said, speaking from the shadows in an unexpectedly warm voice. "That's a nice rose—it really suits you. What can I do for you?" He took his feet off the desk but he remained seated, and shadowed.

Sara felt perversely annoyed with herself when the only thing that she could find to say in response to this greeting was: "How do you know my name?"

"Please sit down, Miss Lindley," the Dragon Man said—and waited until she did so before continuing. "Children are a rare and precious commodity nowadays," the astral tattooist said, softly. "Not just to their elective parents. Did you ever hear the saying that it takes a village to raise a child?"

"Everyone has," Sara told him. She leaned forward, but the lamp was too cleverly-positioned; the Dragon Man's face was as deeply shadowed from this angle as it had been when she was standing up.

"Well, it might have been true once," the Dragon Man told her. "Nowadays, though, it can easily take a whole city. I think you'll find that everybody in town knows your name, Miss Lindley—even people you've never spoken to, and wouldn't recognize if you bumped into them on the street. It's a quiet sort of celebrity, but it's more substantial in its way than anything brokered by TV. You were the only one in your year, you see, this side of Kendal or ManLiv. Think of that! No...don't. It seems quite normal to you, of course—but even people of your parents' ages, let alone mine...." He left the sentence dangling.

Sara remembered the people who had been looking at her earlier that day. She remembered how she had fled from them once, and refused to flee a second time. Would it have made a difference, she wondered, if she'd realized that every one of them, save perhaps for the children, had known her name?

"You know Father Lemuel and Father Gustave," she said, accusingly. "That's how you know my name."

The Dragon Man shook his head slightly, as if to deny that he'd been exaggerating, although the gesture was barely visible. "I haven't seen Lem in twenty years," he said. "Before you were born." But he didn't say it is as if were a denial of her accusation; he said it as if it were something he regretted slightly—as if he should have kept in closer contact with Father Lemuel, but hadn't.

In any case, Sara thought, Father Lemuel's surname wasn't Lindley. She was named after her biological father, according to custom. How would eight parents ever have settled the question of which of them their child ought to be named after, if the custom had been otherwise?

"Everybody takes an interest in children, Miss Lindley," the sublimate technologist said, mistaking her silence for confusion.

"More than you'll understand, until you're a little older." There was a peculiar wistfulness in the old man's tone that made Sara feel uncomfortable.

"Ms. Chatrian says that you're the man to talk to about shadowbats," she said, deciding that it was time to get to the point.

"Very kind of her, I'm sure," the old man said, equably. "Knowing Linda, though, I doubt that she'd be sending you to me if you wanted to order a few extra decorations in a different style. So what about shadowbats?"

"A flock of them came into my room the other night," Sara told him. "They were attracted by the scent of my rose."

The Dragon Man sniffed audibly. "Colibri?" he asked, after a slight pause.

Sara nodded, and the Dragon Man nodded too. "You left your window open expecting hummingbirds," he deduced. "Your first hummingbirds, at a guess. I can see how a flock of shadowbats might have been a disappointment...and a puzzle."

"You don't seem very surprised," Sara observed. "Ms. Chatrian agreed that the perfume might have attracted the bats—a glitch in the new technology, she said—but she didn't believe me when I said that they seemed to be absorbing the scent from the air...and getting drunk on it."

The Dragon Man shifted his position slightly, but he didn't expose his face. He lifted his bony shoulders in what might have been a shrug. His shoulders, unlike Ms. Chatrian's, had no talent at all for expressing contempt. "New technology always does more than it's intended to," he said, pensively. "Shaped sublimates are designed to soak up everything they need from their hosts, but the absorption process is necessarily crude; it's not surprising that they sometimes soak up other things as well. Nobody notices, for the most part, but perfume is...well, more noticeable. You have to remember that they're creatures like none that natural selection ever produced, and that they don't know what they're not supposed to do. They have built-in inhibitions about settling on anyone else's surskin, but fluttering around is the name of their game. You weren't afraid, I hope?"

"Of course not," Sara said. "I knew they couldn't hurt me, even if they touched me, or if I breathed one in—but I wondered if they might be in danger."

The old man shifted in his seat again, as if Sara's story were causing him some slight disturbance, but he clung stubbornly to his protective shadow. *He must have set things up this way to protect his clients from the sight of him,* Sara thought. *But if he's willing to do that, why won't he use the cosmetic potential of his smartsuit?*

"They seemed to be getting drunk, did they?" the Dragon Man murmured, as if he were trying to get the thought more securely into his head. "And you think they might have overdone it, poor things? I don't think they'd readily take aboard anything that would do them harm...but new technology always has unexpected glitches, just as lovely Linda says. Who knows?" He paused for a few moments before adding: "It would be interesting, though, wouldn't it?"

"Would it?" Sara countered.

"Biochemically interesting, I mean. Colibri is a moderately complex cocktail, and the metabolic systems of sublimated quasi-life are straight off the drawing-board, so I doubt if they were ever formally introduced in the lab. It must be idiosyncratic to the flock, though—there are plenty of interaction opportunities in ManLiv, and even more down south. Linda doesn't meddle much with her off-the-shelf products, so the scent must be standard, unless there's been some weird interaction with your personal metabolism—but the shadowbats would be the prime suspects anyhow, given that they're in the earliest stages of their evolution." He stopped, and waited, as if to give Sara the opportunity to complain if the argument were beyond her comprehension.

She was having difficulty following the thread, but she didn't want to admit it." Do you meddle much with off-the-shelf products, Mr. Warburton?" she asked.

"You can call me Frank if I can call you Sara," he said, amiably. "To answer the question, though—yes, I'm an inveterate tinkerer, just like your Father Lem. Old habits die hard, even when you're in unfamiliar territory. I used to do beautiful work, you know, when I was younger. Birds, roses, hearts, mottoes...even dragons with gold and silver scales, like the one in the window, and angels with swans' wings and breath like holy fire—but never Washington crossing the Delaware." He waited a moment to see whether Sara would ask him what he meant by the last remark, but she didn't want to seem ignorant and she knew that she could always ask one of her parents.

"I must be one of the last men alive who worked with needles, on bare skin," the Dragon Man went on. "That's why I keep them in the window, like whiskers dropped from the dragon's snout. I've always kept pace, with the organics and the smartsuits, all the way from...well, not quite the beginning, but at least a time when a few of us were still willing and able to stand naked every time we took a

111

bath or changed our poor dead clothes. I've always meddled, Sara. I carried the habit over when I qualified as a sublimate engineer, just as I'd carried it over into all the other retraining programs I had to go through in order to maintain the outer semblance of my career. I'm older than I look, you know." He smiled to signal that the last comment was a joke, and that he knew exactly how old he looked, when he was clearly visible.

"Do you know who owns the shadowbats that came into my room?" Sara asked. It seemed more diplomatic than asking whether he had meddled with any shadowbats in such a way as to give them an appetite for hummingbird-food.

"I can find out," he replied, confidently. "What do you want me to do about it if I do?"

Sara hesitated. She wasn't sure. "Could you fix them?" she asked, curiously.

"Are you sure they're broken?" he countered. "Perhaps they've acquired a whole new realm of experience, and discovered a brand new pleasure. Fixing them might be cruel, don't you think?"

"They're not hummingbirds," Sara said. "I chose colibri because...." She trailed off, realizing that what she was saying was utterly irrelevant to the question he had posed. Her eyes had adjusted to the poor light now, and she could make out the vague lines of Frank Warburton's features. She was suddenly convinced that was looking at her intently, with a very peculiar expression on his face. She immediately told herself that it must be a trick of the shadows, but she wouldn't be convinced.

She had been told often enough that smartsuits were "emotionally intelligent"—which meant that they were designed to signal and signify, even better than unmasked faces, all the things that people needed to communicate face-to-face but couldn't put into words. Their role was, however, essentially supportive. If the human being within was enigmatic, the extra layers of synthetic skin wouldn't decipher the mystery. Frank Warburton suddenly seemed even more deeply enigmatic than the surrounding shadows forced him to be— more deeply enigmatic than Sara had ever imagined that any human being could seem.

"Do you know, Sara," the old man said, apparently wanting to set her at her ease, "that you're the first customer I've had this morning? On a Saturday! I have four appointments on the machine, but they're all for this evening, after sunset. Why is that, do you think? Is it going to be bats all the way, now? Am I becoming a creature of the dusk myself? Sublimate entities don't have to be shadows, you know. They can be bright, like creatures of pure radiance, or nearly invisible."

"I know," Sara said. "I thought about that. I thought about having a golden dragon fitted to my smartsuit—but my parents would never have let me do it."

"Did you, indeed?" he said, as if he were genuinely impressed. "You'd have come to me, of course—what a fine time we might have had with *that* design. It's not just dragons, though. We can make all manner of fays and phantoms. Imagine that! We could fill the world—the real world, that is, not one of its virtual parallels—with quasi-life that we can't even see. For now, we have shadows, which only fade away in the twilight...but in time, there'll be hosts of angels dancing around us in the broadest daylight, unseen and unsuspected. Or maybe we'll want to reserve the word *angel* for the ones that glow like haloes. Fashion is a fickle thing, but I can't help getting a little bit impatient with it...you can see what I mean, can't you Sara? You really have thought about it."

"I think I can see," she said. "Yes, I really have thought about it. The spiders and the scorpions seem a little silly to me too—but the shadowbats are better, and the potential that's still untapped...what you mean is that you meddle because you're anxious to move on."

"Old age breeds impatience," Frank Warburton told her, as gravely if he were imparting a dark secret. "My kind of old age does, at any rate. You won't find out about your kind for a very long time. I don't frighten you, do I, Sara? I frighten children sometimes. I thought I might have frightened you, last time we met."

"You remember that?" Sara said. It seemed astonishing.

"You were with Stephen and Quilla," he reminded her, as if he felt obliged to provide proof. "I knew you were Lem's girl. If Gus had been with you...or even Maryelle...but maybe not. Did I frighten you?"

"No," Sara said, not quite sure that it was true but wanting it to be. "I was startled, that's all. You didn't have to turn away like that. You could have said hello."

"That's good," he said. "I wish I had said hello, now. Better late than never. Did you tell your parents that you were coming to see me?"

"I didn't know myself," she said. "Actually, I didn't even tell them I was coming to see Ms. Chatrian. I have my own credit account now, so I didn't have to."

"They'll haul you up in front of a committee of enquiry as soon as you get home, regardless," the Dragon Man observed. "If there's one thing parents hate, it's not being kept informed.... I can even remember that, you see, even though it's been more than a hundred years since I was a parent, and more than two hundred since...well, it's probably best not go into that. You can tell them all that I've promised to look into your little mystery, and that I'll do my very best to solve the problem. Just between you and me, it might not be easy, but I'll try. I have to respect client confidentiality, you understand, but I'll certainly try to figure out what's happened, and what can be done about it. Will you trust me to take care of it?"

"I suppose so," Sara said, lamely. She waited for him to say something else, but he didn't. He was as still as a statue now, and she had the feeling that he wanted her to go.

She stood up, a little unsteadily. He remained silent.

"Well," she said, "I suppose...goodbye, then. She turned towards the door, but she moved slowly, in case he called her back. He didn't get up.

It wasn't until the door slid open that he spoke again. "If ever you need a new suit, Miss Lindley," the seated Dragon Man said, his tone barely above a whisper, "you might want to look further afield than Linda Chatrian. She's a little behind the times. But the rose does suit you. You made a good choice."

Sara paused on the threshold to look back over her shoulder. "Thanks" she said—but Frank Warburton was no longer looking in her direction. His face was still invisible, but his head had slumped forward, so that he seemed to be staring at the keypad on his desk.

It didn't occur to her until the door had closed behind her that perhaps Frank Warburton hadn't been quite ready to say goodbye either, but that he simply hadn't felt capable of continuing the conversation as comfortably as he wished. For a moment or two she considered going back into the shop to ask if he was all right, but she guessed readily enough that if he really had wanted her to go, he certainly wouldn't want her to return.

Sara realized, a trifle belatedly, that she had been telling the truth, even though politeness would have compelled her to lie. She hadn't been frightened of the Dragon Man—not this time, at any rate. She hadn't been frightened at all. She didn't know him well enough to know whether she liked him, but she felt—however absurdly—that they had something in common. She and he were both exceptional. She and he were so exceptional that everybody knew their names, and recognized them whenever and wherever they happened to be.

She resolved to talk to the Dragon Man about that, when—not if—she saw him again.

Given that he was so much older than she was, she thought, he might be able to give her one or two pointers on being exceptional that even Father Lemuel hadn't yet had occasion to master.

CHAPTER XVI

That night, Sara left her window wide open again. It was simple curiosity—or so she told herself. She wanted to make sure that what she'd told the tailor and the sublime technologist was really true: that the shadowbats were indeed intoxicating themselves on the evaporating nectar of her rose. She also wanted to take a longer look at the shadowbats themselves, in order to appreciate the ingenuity and the workmanship that had gone into the new kind of life.

She didn't have long to wait, and felt a thrill of pleasure when she saw them emerge from the night. They knew the way, now; they knew she had a rose, and what it could do for them.

There were six of them, and Sara had no doubt that they were the same ones. She wondered, as she watched them fluttering around the room, whether they had returned to the hometree on all the nights when she had kept her window closed, hovering invisibly outside the plastic and waiting forlornly for a treat that never came, or whether this was the first time they had been allowed out since their mysterious temporary disappearance.

Either way, she realized, the further encouragement that she was now providing would only serve to reinforce their new habit. They would surely come back again and again, whether she condescended to let them in or not

She lay still on the bed, with the rose fully extended, carefully watching the aerobatic display of the living shadows and measuring its quality. Having made their way around the bedroom twenty or thirty times, following incredibly intricate trajectories—presumably mopping up the molecules that had permeated the atmosphere before their arrival—the six phantom bats eventually came into a more orderly formation. They straightened out their courses, taking turns to skim the surface of the flower. They came from three different angles, cutting graceful arcs through the space above the flower. The

116

arcs intersected at a point above the central style, from whose base the perfume was released.

They were perfectly coordinated, as if they were operating as a practiced team rather than a mere haphazard flock. They never seemed to be in the least danger of colliding, even though their flight was becoming more excited, and their speed was increasing. The scent emitted by the rose was no longer perceptible in her own nostrils; it was vanishing from the air almost as soon as it evaporated.

Were the shadowbats really getting drunk, Sara wondered, or was that merely the best analogy she could draw? It wasn't a helpful one, in any case. She had never been drunk herself, and had never seen any of her parents drunk—they were very careful about setting a bad example while they were at home. All she knew about drunkenness was based on TV shows she had seen—mostly comedies, at that. She had no idea what being drunk felt like. She imagined it as a combination of dizziness and pleasurable excitement, a matter of getting *carried away*.

Sara had only ever been "carried away" by sheer excitement, and she realized as she watched the aerial display that it was something she no longer experienced very frequently. Without being quite aware of it, she had "grown out of" the capacity to laugh until she cried when she was tickled or chased...and it was possible that what the phantoms were experiencing was nothing like that at all. Perhaps it was more like the greed that sometimes inspired her to eat sweet things too quickly...or the sense of triumphant achievement she had felt, all too briefly, the day she had climbed the hometree.

That too, she realized, was something she had not felt for quite a while, although she couldn't believe that it was something people grew out of, the way they lost the knack of being tickled to hysteria.

Perhaps, Sara thought, the effect of the perfume on the shadowbats was more like the drugs she had been warned about in school—but she found it hard to believe that such frail phantoms were capable of hallucination, or being interested in any hallucinations they might chance to experience.

The idea of a shadowbat, or a flock of shadowbats, lying down in a cocoon so that they could visit a fantasy world or take some kind of training program was absurd enough to bring a smile to Sara's face. But was it really so absurd? If the shadowbats' sensory apparatus was so much simpler than her own, wouldn't that make it easier for them to be fooled by simulatory input?

Perhaps, she dared to think, shadowbats didn't need hoods or cocoons, or even picture windows, to look out into alternative worlds. Perhaps they only needed an appropriate scent...perhaps, when they breathed colibri, they were transformed in their own tiny minds into hummingbirds, or dragons, or things of which only bats or phantoms were capable of dreaming....

It was all unbelievable—but Sara felt strangely proud of herself for having been able to imagine it, and wondered if Father Lemuel would be proud of her too, if she told him about it. She had no plans to tell him yet, of course; the sensation of having a real secret, much more personal and profound than the secret of her experiment in dragonflight, was far too precious. In time, though, when Mr. Warburton had found a solution to the puzzle and a means of tackling the problem, it might be enjoyable to talk the whole thing over with Father Lemuel....

Sara suddenly realized that the flight of the shadows was become ever more rapid, and their turns ever more hectic—and that as they gave themselves up to sheer madness, their uncertain shapes were becoming even more uncertain, less obviously bat-like.

It was as if the sublimate creatures were attempting some strange metamorphosis that they were not yet able to contrive; as if they were no longer content to be shadowbats, but wanted to be shadow-caterpillars, or shadow-tadpoles, on their way to becoming shadow-butterflies or shadow-frogs.

The limits of absurdity seemed to stretch then, as Sara found it abruptly possible to believe what she had not been able to believe before, to accept as an evident fact what had seemed a ridiculous fancy only a few moments ago.

Now, she was almost ready to be convinced that the vaporous creatures really did nurture a primitive hope that drinking their fill of volatilized colibri might actually turn them into hummingbirds, endowing them with marvelous brightness and color instead of their fugitive mock-darkness. What was actually happening to them, though, was that they were beginning to break up under the strain—to dissipate like curls of smoke.

If they continued, Sara felt sure that their "skins" would disintegrate, and whatever internal organization they had would decay into chaos.

Sara became suddenly anxious. She did not want the shadowbats to come to any harm—and even if they succeeded in reforming, in transforming themselves into something else, that was surely a far more dangerous business than merely "getting drunk".

Her desire to know and understand what was happening was still increasing, but so was her fear that something bad might be happening, and that it would be her fault.

Acting on an urgent impulse, Sara sat up on the bed and swung her legs over the side. Her abrupt movement sent the invaders scattering in every direction.

She leapt to the floor and ran to her cupboard. As soon as the door slid sideways she rummaged among the clutter that had accumulated on the cupboard's narrow floor, until she found an ancient screw-topped jar in which her younger self—who seemed by now to have been a very different person—had stored her kaleidobubbles.

The gelatin spheres had become sticky with age. When she tried to pour them out they resisted, clinging together in a stubborn adhesive mass, but Sara poked her forefinger into the jar to break up the mass, and shook the inverted jar as hard as she could. She persisted until she had dislodged them all, pouring them out into the shower-nook.

When the jar was empty, except for a few smears of translucent color on the inner surface of the clear plastic, she started chasing the shadowbats with the empty jar.

The dark phantoms evaded her amateurish scooping without the slightest difficulty, even though they were still confused and over-excited. They no longer seemed to be disintegrating, now that the flow of nectar had been interrupted, but the perfume of the flower was still diffusing into the air, and Sara had to suppose that the process had only been slowed down.

Realizing that she was going about her task in the wrong way, Sara lay down on the bed again and stretched herself out in a supine position. She lay quite still, and waited for the shadowbats to begin moving more purposefully again.

Gradually, she eased the open neck of the jar closer and closer to the rim of the rose's ring of petals. She only needed to adjust its position two or three times before the momentum of a giddy dive sent one of the shadow-creatures straight into the trap. She had the lid in place within half a second, and screwed down it tight. She jumped down off the bed again, delighted with her success.

The captive shadowbat only needed a couple of minutes to measure out the dimensions of its cell, and to discover that there was no escape therefrom. Then it settled on the glass, positioned over one of the translucent smears as if it were a paint-daubed image. It did not move again.

The five remaining fliers seemed to realize that something was amiss. They fluttered around the nightlight as if they were taking account of their number and fretting over its inadequacy. Then, very suddenly, they shot out of the window into the night, and were gone.

Sara followed them, but they were invisible in the darkness. She had no idea which way they had gone.

"Is there anyone there?" she called, tentatively. She did not dare to shout, in case her parents heard her—although she realized soon enough that there was little prospect of that, given that the hometree was carefully designed to protect its residents from extraneous and unwelcome noises. She filled her lungs again, ready to repeat the question, but then she thought better of it, and let her breath out silently.

It was too silly. If someone *were* there, lurking behind the garden hedge, they would not reply to her call. Nor was there any real reason to expect that anyone *would* be there. The shadowbats might have flown for a kilometer or more, from any direction.

She stared out into the darkness for half a minute, pensively weighing the jar in her left hand. Then she closed the window, gently.

She went to her desktop and called up the local directory. When she had found the number she wanted she typed out a text message, taking care to avoid using conventional abbreviations or making any spelling mistakes. MR WARBURTON, the message read, I'VE CAPTURED ONE OF THE DRUNKEN SHADOWBATS. I'LL BRING IT TO YOU IN THE MORNING, SO THAT YOU CAN EXAMINE IT. SARA LINDLEY. After a moment's hesitation, she pressed the SEND button.

She hesitated for several seconds more, her fingers hovering uncertainly above the keypad as she wondered what to do for the best.

The spirit of far play eventually moved her to log on to the local noticeboard and post a hastily-typed public message, which read: IF 1 OF 6 SHADOWBATS MISSING, DON'T WORRY. IS SAFE. NOT STOLEN. WILL RELEASE, OR TELL U WHERE U CAN COLLECT, SOON AS CHECK OUT ANOMALY IN ITS BEHAVIOUR. She knew that she ought to amend the final sentence in the interests of clarity, but eventually decided that it would serve its purpose. She also thought about signing the message, but decided not to. After all, she didn't know who she was writing to, so why should he—or she—know who the message was coming from?

THE DRAGON MAN, BY BRIAN STABLEFORD

Satisfied, in the end, that she had done everything she needed to do, for the time being, Sara left the jar on her desk and went back to bed. She carefully smoothed her rose flat so that she could sleep unhindered by any further inconvenience.

CHAPTER XVII

When Sara got up the next morning and wandered absent-mindedly into the communal dining room she found all of her parents waiting for her—even Father Lemuel. She knew as soon as she stepped through the door that she was in trouble.

"What did I do?" she asked, although she knew well enough that trapping the shadowbat was likely to be the last straw that had broken the proverbial camel's back. She was quick to add: "How did you know? Is my room being monitored? Or are you just keeping track of my mail?"

"The resident AI is programmed to take note of any-thing...unusual," Father Gustave told her, having the grace to look slightly shamefaced about it.

"We already knew about your visit to the astral tattooist, of course," Mother Maryelle put in.

"How?" Sara waned to know, having decided that she had a right to be annoyed. "Did he tell you—or Ms. Chatrian? What happened to client confidentiality?"

"It wasn't either of them," Father Stephen assured her. "We didn't need any human informants, although...well, perhaps you didn't realize how much notice people would take of your movements if they saw you without us. Not just people we know, or other parents—everybody."

Sara was speechless, but she knew that her expression must speak volumes.

"It's not that they're *spying*," Mother Verena said, defensively.

"People talk, you see," Father Gustave said, hastening to take up the burden of explanation, "and they need things to talk about. After the weather, politics and the march of technology, children are a favorite topic. Anybody's children."

"It's perfectly understandable," Mother Maryelle added. "Now that people are directly involved in parenting for such a tiny fraction of their adult lifespan, it's only natural that they take a greater interest in children they're only indirectly involved with."

"'Indirectly' meaning any that they see, even on an occasional basis, or any whose existence they know anything at all about," Father Stephen put in, presumably intending to be helpful—although the way that Father Gustave scowled suggested that he wasn't at all grateful for the pedantic definition.

Sara remembered what the Dragon Man had said about it taking a whole city to raise a child nowadays. She realized, belatedly, that he hadn't meant to imply that the child needed the city, but rather that the city needed the child. Ms. Mapledean and Father Lemuel had both taken the trouble to explain to her that the Population Bureau was reluctant to grant child-rearing licenses to more than eight co-parents, partly because larger groups were notoriously prone to premature disintegration and partly because of the supposed limitation of a child's primary-bonding capacity. Until this moment, she had left the fact unconsidered, like the vast majority of the facts her teachers and parents rained ceaselessly down upon her, but now she found herself rudely confronted with one of the more obvious implications of the policy.

"You mean," she said, as the prospect became clear to her for the first time, "that wherever I go, and whatever I do, people won't be content just to watch me go by... they'll report it all back to you."

"It's not a matter of *reporting back*," Father Stephen said. "Not in a sneaky way...."

"It's more a matter of wanting to ask questions...," Mother Jolene put in, before she was interrupted in her turn.

"In any case, it's not something to worry about," Mother Quilla took over. "It's discreet, and it won't last forever. In three or four years time—sooner if you grow as fast as I did—you'll be indistinguishable from an adult by sight alone. You'll become far less visible, or at least far less noticeable. You're entering a difficult phase just now. Perhaps we should have warned...."

"Perhaps we should at least have talked to you about it," Mother Verena said, effortlessly taking up the relay baton despite Mother Quilla's obvious reluctance to relinquish it, "but we thought it would make you more self-conscious if it were actually pointed out, so we...."

"None of which is relevant to the matter in hand," Father Gustave broke in, testily. "Which is that *you* should be keeping us informed, so we wouldn't have to rely on second hand information."

"We gave you every chance to tell us," Father Aubrey pointed out. "We didn't say anything at all yesterday, thinking that you'd probably feel able to tell us everything today, when you'd had a chance to sleep on it...."

"But this is simply too much," Father Stephen said. "You can't go around setting traps for other people's bodywear. It's not even legal, let alone moral."

Sara was still trying to work out who might have said what to whom, and when, but the change of subject forced her to abandon that train of thought and deflect her attention to the question of why, if her parents knew about the captured shadowbat, they hadn't taken the trouble to interfere at the time. If, as Father Gustave said, the hometree's Artificial Intelligence was programmed to take note of anything unusual, it was presumably also programmed only to wake them up in case of emergency. If this didn't qualify as an emergency, at least by the programmed standards of the resident AI, the trouble she was in couldn't be very bad.

"I can explain...," she began—but her parents were too anxious to get their own thoughts on record to allow her to complete the statement. Even though she was used to it, the interruption annoyed her. If her parents weren't even going to listen to her explanation, she thought, what was the point of the hastily-convened meeting? Were they just taking the opportunity to let off steam themselves?

"Actually, Steve," Mother Maryelle said, "we're perfectly entitled, in law, to capture any stray creature that wanders into our house, and I really don't think that Sara's action can be classified as *immoral*...."

Sara watched the expressions on her other parents' faces change as they realized that Mother Maryelle was playing the lawyer yet again—but she was careful to keep her own face straight.

"This isn't about the legality of catching the shadowbat, Maryelle," Mother Quilla interrupted, recklessly. "It's about trust. It's about Sara keeping us informed of what she's doing...."

"It isn't about that either," Mother Jolene put in. "The real issue, to my mind, is the matter of recklessly posting notices on the public boards...."

"To my mind...," Father Aubrey began—but he didn't have time to finish before Father Gustave used the power of his baritone voice to shout for quiet.

"This is not the way to go about things," Father Gustave said, when he finally had everyone's grudging attention. "Sara, would you like to tell us what's going on?"

It's about time, Sara thought, all apologetic impulses having evaporated like the scent from her rose. "You all seem to know far more about what's going on than I do," she said, not quite succeeding in ridding her tone of sarcasm. "I didn't know that I had to call a house-meeting before leaving the hometree, and I thought you might be pleased that I was using my initiative instead of asking one of you to sort out a problem with a rose that I chose and paid for. It's no big thing. Shadowbats aren't supposed to be attracted by my rose, and they certainly aren't supposed to be getting high on its nectar, so I thought I'd better grab one while I could so that the Drag—I mean, Mr. Warburton—could check it out and report back to the manufacturer. It's not exactly kidnapping, is it?"

She counted five deep frowns, but no one took her to task for her combative attitude.

"No," said Father Gustave, who still had the floor, "it's not kidnapping. I assume that we can take Maryelle's word that it's not a crime at all, in spite of Steve's anxieties. The whole thing is just a slight failure of diplomacy. Do you know whose shadowbats they are?"

"No," Sara retorted. "Do you?"

"Not yet," Father Gustave admitted. "I dare say that we can find out easily enough. Has the Drag—I mean, Mr. Warburton—replied to your message yet?"

Sara checked her wristpad, then said; "No. There's no response to the message on the board, either. But it's early—and it's Sunday."

"Then you'd better give the jar to me," Father Gustave said. "I'll take it from here."

"It's Sunday," Sara repeated.

"What does that have to do with anything?" Father Gustave demanded. He was obviously making heroic efforts to hold his irritation in check; having seized control of the argument, he was under an obligation to handle it responsibly.

"There's no school today," Sara said. "I can take it to the Dragon Man myself. He'll know what to do with it."

Father Gustave opened his mouth to reply, but was overtaken by a sudden fit of doubt. His eyes flickered from side to side—not so much in search of support, Sara guessed, as to make sure that he still had a license to speak for everyone. The moment he surrendered the conversational initiative, though, he was swamped. "No, you can't," said Mother Quilla and Father Aubrey, in unison, while Father Stephen was saying "I don't think that's a good idea," Mother Jolene "Shouldn't one of us go with you?" and Father Lemuel "Well I'm glad that's settled."

Sara saw Mother Maryelle waiting patiently for the cacophony to decay into muttering chaos, choosing exactly the right moment to raise her own voice above the fading hubbub to say: "Your credit won't stretch to another two-way cab ride to Blackburn, Sara. I'm surprised it stretched to one, after what you paid for that rose."

Sara had momentarily forgotten her budget problems. She had already realized that her newly-granted freedom to handle her own finances had its downside, but she hadn't expected to hit the rocks quite so soon. "These are special circumstances," she said, rallying her argumentative reserves. "I mean, this is a new technology displaying an unexpected side-effect. I'm the one who discovered it. It could be news. National news, even."

"As we've been trying to explain, Sara," Mother Quilla said, with an affected world-weariness that didn't suit her at all, "everything you do that's at all out of the ordinary is news, at least locally—and not in a good way."

"Not necessarily in a bad way, though," Mother Jolene was quick to put in.

"Exactly," said Sara, seeing an opportunity and moving swiftly to seize it. "Don't you think it would reflect better on you, as parents, if I...."

"Don't you dare take that tone...," Father Aubrey began, at exactly the same time as Mother Quilla said "That's not your...," and Father Stephen said "That's not the point at...."

None of them got to finish, because Father Gustave was lying in wait for another opportunity to play the tyrant; he shouted for quiet again.

"Oh, shut up yourself, Gus," Father Lemuel said, brutally. "She's right, damn it. Nothing's likely to win us prizes from the self-appointed jury of our peeping peers that passes judgment on our every move, but we can at least try not to look stupid. I'll pay for the cab if Sara wants to take the thing to Frank's shop by herself—the important thing is to get it out of our cabbage-patch and make it someone else's problem. Is everybody okay with that?"

Mother Quilla began to say "I don't think...," but it was her eyes that were flickering from side to side now. The words died on her lips as she found no conspicuous support for a tough line.

"Lem's right," said Mother Verena, although Sara guessed that she said it as much to get in a dig at Father Gustave as for any other reason.

"Well, all right," said Father Aubrey. "Jo has a point when she says that not all news is bad, and Sara has a point about showing initiative. And we did all agree that it was time she took a little responsibility for herself. Let's not get hung up about a cab fare to town. Gus?"

"If you think so," Father Gustave said, stiffly.

"Well," Father Lemuel repeated, with grim determination, "I'm glad that's settled."

"But we still need...," Mother Maryelle began.

"Save it for the regular meeting," Father Lemuel said. "Give my regards to Frank, Sara. Tell him it's been far too long—my fault entirely. I'll drop in on him one of these days, when I'm not too busy."

Sara observed several sneers forming in response to Father Lemuel's remark about being too busy, but all of them were politely suppressed before flowering into expressions of open contempt. "I'll have my breakfast first," she said. "In my room, if that's okay." In the absence of any manifest dispute, she assumed that she was free to go, and she wasted no time at all in turning on her heel.

While she ate her breakfast she called Gennifer. Their conversation about the total unreasonableness of parents far outlasted the meal, and might have gone on for a great deal longer if Sara's desktop hadn't posted a flag telling her that she had a message from Frank Warburton waiting to be read.

Sara pasted the message into a window and reported its contents to Gennifer. "*You shouldn't have done that*," she read aloud, "*but since you have, you'd better bring it in as soon as you can. Text me an ETA. Give my regards to Lem, Gus and the others and say 'long time no see'. See you soon. Frank Warburton.*"

"Very Frank," Gennifer observed. "Fancy your Fathers and Mothers knowing a tattooist. If it's been a long time, they must have known him when he really was a tattooist, working on skin instead of smartsuit flesh."

"I don't think they can have known him *that* long ago," Sara said, wishing that she'd done some research into the likely sequence of Mr. Warburton's artistic technologies. "Before all this sublimate stuff, obviously—but there must have been lots of other things between that and using needles to drill ink into *naked flesh*. Smart cellulite, migratory chromocytes, lepidopteran alate scaling...."

"Bioluminescent auras," Gennifer added, not wanting to be left out of the list-making, "metaspectral melanin, dermal ivory inlays...."

Sara knew that Gennifer's suggestions must have been plucked almost at random from ads on the more exotic shopping channels—the ones she and Gennifer supposedly weren't allowed to watch—because that was where she'd borrowed a couple of her examples from, but she daren't challenge Gennifer to tell her what any of the terms meant for fear of instant retaliation.

"I don't have time to gossip, Gen," Sara said, imperiously. "I have important things to do." It seemed like something she had been waiting all her life to say—or, at least, to say with real meaning.

CHAPTER XVIII

As usual, the traffic management system compelled the robocab to let Sara out at the corner of the square most distant from Mr. Warburton's shop, so Sara had to walk diagonally across the open space towards the fire-fountain. No less than six groups of parents had brought infant offspring of various ages to look at the fountain—surely a record for a Sunday morning in Blackburn—and they formed a crowd so large and dense that the children had to be held aloft in order to watch the cascade of sparks. Even so, Sara didn't feel nearly as conspicuous as she had the day before. With that sort of competition, she told herself, no one was likely to be staring at a teenager.

Frank Warburton was waiting for her. He was standing up behind his desk, so his face was no longer in shadow. Sara felt a slight shock, not so much because his face seemed so gaunt and twisted but because his whole body was so very thin and frail. Had he been as thin as that four years earlier, when she'd seen him in Old Manchester? She couldn't be sure. She pulled herself together, determined not to let the least trace of horror or alarm show on her face as she met his eyes.

"Hello again, Miss Lindley," the Dragon Man said, very mildly. He had apparently forgotten their agreement to call one another by their first names.

"I'm sorry to inconvenience you, Mr. Warburton," she said, stiffly, "but I thought it would help you to figure out what had gone wrong if I brought you one of the shadowbats."

The sublimate engineer took the jar from her and peered at the dormant shadowbat. "What's the colored stuff on the walls?" he asked.

"My kaleidobubbles must have leaked," Sara said, apologetically. "They were in there for a long time. It won't have harmed the shadowbat, will it?"

The Dragon Man shrugged his bony shoulders. "If the perfume of your rose has weird effects, who knows what the decay products of old kaleidobubbles might do?" he said. "Can't tell anything by looking. I'll probably need to do a complete proteonomic analysis, although I might be able to narrow the possibilities down with a quick gel-spread. Do you want to watch?"

Sara was mildly surprised by the invitation, which she accepted with alacrity. She was in no hurry to go back home again.

"Better come through, then," he said, leading the way into an inner room.

Sara wasn't surprised to discover that the sublimate technologist's workshop had as little in common with Linda Chatrian's consulting-room as his reception area had with the tailor's. Some of the labtop equipment was similar, although Frank Warburton had nothing like the vats where the tailor grew her embryonic smartsuits or the suspension-clambers where she fitted them. Whatever he meant by a "gel-spread", he obviously didn't do it in the kind of tank in which Sara had been laid out while the winding stem of her rose had integrated itself into her surskin.

Ms. Chatrian liked whiteskin walls and a lightly-perfumed but reassuringly sterile atmosphere; she also favored extra-large windowscreens and Morris chairs upholstered in royal blue and chocolate brown. In stark contrast, the Dragon Man's walls and furniture were stone dead, and his wallscreens were more like portholes than casement windows. Unlike Ms. Chatrian, the Dragon Man obviously liked shelves. He had lots of shelves, many of them filled with jars charged with what looked like colored smoke but obviously wasn't. The air was loaded with a rich cocktail of barely-perceptible odors—as was only to be expected, given the lack of smart walls— and there was more clutter piled up in each and every corner than Sara had ever had in her cupboard, giving the room a curiously rounded aspect. The labtops were clean, though, and the equipment to which the Dragon Man turned his attention seemed to be ready-primed and set to go.

Sara half-expected the shadowbat to make a bid for freedom as soon as the screw-top of the jar was removed, but it remained quiescent. It had to be prompted with the point of a long needle before it would condescend to slide on to a gelatinous sheet in the bottom of a rectangular tray. After waiting for a couple of minutes, Mr. Warburton coaxed it on to a rag of synthetic skin. Sara saw that it had left an imprint on the gel, like a ghostly shadow—or, given that it was a shadow of sorts itself, a ghost of a ghost.

"Sit down," the Dragon Man said to Sara.

In the absence of Morris chairs, Sara had no alternative but to perch on a stool beside the rag. She looked down at the shadowbat, hoping that it would be all right. She wondered whether it was feeding, and whether it would be able to fly again once it had.

In the meantime, the Dragon Man laid a paper-thin sheet of something soft and white over the shadow on the gel in order to take yet another, even fainter, imprint. This one he carefully rolled up; then he set the scroll on the edge of another rectangular bath of gel. This bath was fitted with a cluster of external wires and numerous dials. Three eye-like red circles were lit up as he tripped a hidden switch.

Mr. Warburton watched the placid surface for two minutes, although nothing as happening to it that Sara could detect. Then he went back to the first imprint, whose supportive medium had now become so viscous as almost to have set hard. This time, the Dragon Man used a scalpel to cut out the imprint, and a broad spatula to lift it from the tray. He slid the near-solid lump into a beaker half-full of another viscous liquid, into which it seemed to dissolve entirely. Then he poured a measure of the solution into the maw of a pot-bellied machine which put Sara in mind of the inorganic parts of the hometree's plumbing systems—the parts that were so ugly they were tastefully hidden away in the cellar. Nothing now remained in the gel-bath but a cartoonish cut-out, which was only slightly reminiscent of a bat with extended wings.

"Right," said the Dragon Man, pulling another stool from under the bench so that he could sit down too. "The full proteonome analysis will take at least four hours, probably six, even though the poor little devil only has a few dozen pseudogenes. The chromotrace should tell if there's anything untoward going on, though, and ought to offer a few clues as to how and why...." He broke off as he seemed to realize, suddenly, that Sara didn't understand what he was telling her. "Sorry," he said. "Just a second."

His fingers danced on a virtual keyboard projected on the desk in front of one of the wallscreens, which was displaying a series of diagrams far more complicated than anything Sara had yet studied in school. She did her best to look as if she were capable of taking an intelligent interest.

"Right," the Dragon Man said. "It's getting on with the job. There's time to explain, if I'm up to it. Do you know what a proteonome is?"

Sara shook her head.

"What about a genome?"

"It's a set of genes," Sara said. "Chromosomes. DNA. A set of instructions for making a person—or an animal."

"That's right. Every genome has an equivalent proteonome—the full set of proteins that its genes can produce. Some genes work in collaboration, you see, to produce whole populations of related proteins. Different sets of genes are active in different kinds of cells, producing different sets of proteins, so that tissues and organs can do different jobs within the body. When I was born, human bodies had to get by with the genes and proteins that nature provided, but you and I are both equipped with several extra sets. Your smartsuit has the most obvious one, but various bits of your internal technology have minigenomes of their own. It's not as marvelous as it might seem—pre-Crash humans had resident bacteria, and every cell had mitochondria with genes of their own, as well as the genes in the chromosomes. We've just taken the process a little further. Are you with me so far?"

Sara didn't feel that a mere nod was sufficient, so she tried to anticipate the next step in the argument. "And the shadowbat's just an extra bit of smartsuit, or an extra piece of IT," she said. "Another genome, another pre-pro...."

"Proteonome," the Dragon Man finished for her, as her tongue faltered over the unfamiliar word. "That's right—except that DNA isn't equipped to produce vaporous entities, so what the shadowbat has instead makes up what we call pseudogenes...although they still produce proteins, so we can still talk about its proteonome without having to modify the term, even though many of the proteins have never been generated before by natural or artificial genomes. Sorry, that's probably unnecessarily complicated. To cut a long story short, although sublimate organisms—astral tattoos, in the advertising jargon—have gone through all the standard tests to make sure that they're safe to wear, that doesn't mean that every possible interaction between shadowbat proteins and the proteins produced by natural and artificial genomes has been investigated. There's still scope for surprises, especially when one new technology comes into contact with another."

"Just because it's safe for us to wear shadowbats," Sara said, looking down at the dark patch on the rag of synthetic skin, "it doesn't mean that it's safe for the shadowbats to be worn."

"That's true," the Dragon Man conceded. "Sublimate organisms—sublimate just means that they can pass from the solid to the vaporous state without going through a liquid phase, by the way—are rather delicate. It may not have been very wise for the owner of the flock you encountered to let them stray. Having said that, though, there hasn't been any previous report of shadowbats reacting oddly to colibri nectar. I checked that very carefully. Which probably means that someone—probably me—has altered these particular shadowbats in such a way as to open up the possibility."

"Why would you—or someone else—have done that?" Sara asked, warily.

"I'm not the only inveterate tinkerer in the world," Frank Warburton said, defensively. "Everyone does it. Everyone with an atom of curiosity. Anyhow, although the full analysis will take a few hours, tickling the secondary trace with a little electricity in this bath here will separate the organic compounds into a line-spectrum, like the ones police scientists and the newsvids call genetic fingerprints. Comparing that to the print the bat is supposed to produce should tell us in a matter of twenty or thirty minutes whether there is an anomaly, and might offer a clue as to its nature. Until then we might as well make polite conversation. Your parents know about the shadowbat, I suppose?"

"Oh yes," said Sara. "They also know about every move I made yesterday."

"Ah," the Dragon Man murmured. "The old jungle telegraph. It never fails to deliver the news. Are they annoyed with me too?"

"I don't think so," Sara reassured him. "Father Lemuel sent you his best wishes, and he wouldn't have done that if he'd been annoyed. In fact, he wouldn't have persuaded the others to let me bring the shadowbat in if he'd been seriously annoyed with either of us. I think it was more a matter of them thinking that they had to make a point."

"That's understandable," the Dragon Man observed, obviously feeling that he ought to be supportive of Sara's parents. "Do you mind if I send Lem a message to let him know I've invited you to wait for the preliminary results of my inquiry? I don't want your parents to worry."

"Not at all," Sara replied, politely. She waited until he had dispatched the text message before saying: "Can I ask you a personal question?"

"About my horrid face?"

Sara blinked in surprise. "No!" she said. "No...it was just...well, as you've known Father Lemuel for such a long time, and as you knew my name before ever seeing me...I wanted to ask you whether you knew the man I was named after—Gerard Lindley, my biological father?"

It was the Dragon Man's turn to look surprised. "Why would I?" he blurted out. "Sorry...I mean, no, I don't think so. Do you have some reason to think that I might have known him?"

"Not really," Sara confessed. "I suppose it's because I don't know very much about him myself, except that he lived in these parts during his later years, that I thought you might...although I suppose Father Lemuel might have mentioned it, if he thought...sorry. It's just that most of the kids in my class know quite a bit about their biological parents, because at least some of their parents knew them when they were alive. I've asked my parents why they decided to look after the child of people they didn't know, but all they said was that someone had to look after the children of parents that nobody knew, and they'd decided it was a good thing to do. There doesn't seem to be any record of my biological mother at all, because she died during the Crash, and all I can find out about my biological father is his name, dates and some of his places of residence. He didn't live very long, but he didn't die till 2161. That's long before Father Lemuel was born but...you were alive then, weren't you?"

"Yes I was," Mr. Warburton answered, softly. "So it's not beyond the bounds of possibility that I did meet your biological father, even though I can't remember it. He could even have been a customer—all my records of that era are long-lost. Your parents are right, you know. A great many people deposited sperm and eggs during the Crash, not knowing whether they'd ever be used—or even whether there'd be anyone around to use them. If today's parents all insisted on exercising the rights of people they knew personally, the genetic heritage of most of the Crash's victims would be lost. You've probably been told in school that loss of genetic variety within a species is always a bad thing, but modern genetic engineering can cope with the practical problems—what's really at stake is a point of principle."

"The right to found a family," Sara said, to demonstrate that she could easily keep up with this phase of the conversation.

"There was a time, during the Crash, when we thought everybody might have lost that right," the old man told her, in a somber tone.

Sara knew that, of course, as a bare fact—she had been informed of it at least once by nearly every adult she had ever come into contact with—but this was the first time that any of her informants had ever been able to mean "we" in a more literal sense than "the human race". Frank Warburton had actually lived through the latter years of the Crash.

Sara waited for him to go on.

CHAPTER XIX

"I was born a little too early to be a miracle child myself," the Dragon Man said, with a faint sigh. "The plague of sterility was running riot, but children were still being born, and the panic hadn't yet extinguished hope that cures could be found to make the infertile fertile again. The banks of sperm and eggs still seemed to most of us to be a precautionary measure—something we'd only have to fall back on if the worst came to the worst, and just to help out for a while even then."

Sara nodded, to let him know that she understood what he was saying, and wanted him to continue.

"When I was your age—that would be 2112 or so, I guess—we had no idea that the historians of the future would decide that the Crash was already completed and that we were already into the Aftermath. We didn't know that there were too many different viruses, or that too many of them had already wormed their way permanently into the genome. We didn't understand that the old world had already ended. Imagine that! The world as we knew it was finished, and we didn't even know. Our own parents...our own biological parents...were still trying to save it. Except, I suppose, for those who were still trying to destroy it. Do they tell you in school that the plagues came out of biological warfare labs, or have they drawn a polite curtain over that sort of thing?"

"I think they tell us the truth," Sara said, slightly shocked by the idea that they might not. "Ms. Mapledean says there's no way to be sure of the origin of any particular virus, because they were mutating so quickly and no one ever admitted to anything, but that it was definitely a war of sorts."

"Of sorts," the Dragon Man echoed. "That's right. Sorts that people had never been able to fight before. At least you had to meet your enemy face to face when people used to fight with clubs and swords—you even had to know who he was. In a plague war, every-one who hasn't had the right injections becomes an enemy by de-fault...and nobody had *all* the right injections, no matter who he was or how deep his bunker might be. Anyway, no one had actually ac-cepted the fact, as yet, that the world would have to be comprehen-sively reinvented and totally redesigned. No one had yet grasped the fact that no human female would be able to bear a child of her own for...I don't know how long. I suppose we could put the clock back, now, if we ever wanted to. We have the technology now—but we didn't have it during the Aftermath.

"I don't remember there being a day, or a year, when we all recognized that things had changed forever. It crept up on us. Artifi-cial wombs were designed, perfected, used...but there wasn't a point in time when everybody accepted that they weren't just a stopgap, or an emergency measure. We kept on anticipating a future that never came, until the realization dawned that we'd been living in a new world for decades, and that it was now *the* world, a way of life we were stuck with. It was evolution, not revolution, too gradual to be clearly perceived.

"The natural miracle children became rarer and rarer, and the technological miracle children gradually became commonplace. I suppose they teach you in school that it all worked out for the best, that it was necessary as well as lucky—and so it was—but it didn't seem like that when we were living through it. We lived it as trag-edy, and those of us who are left still remember it that way."

"But it *was* necessary," Sara murmured, when the old man looked for a response.

"Yes, it was," he agreed. "In a world where everyone might live to be three hundred, or three thousand, it's necessary as well as po-lite that we should all postpone the exercise of our right to have children—our right of replacement—until we're dead. It's the only way we can live on the Earth without bringing about another ecoca-tastrophe even worse than the Crash. It's the way it has to be."

"And it *was* lucky," Sara added, echoing what Ms. Mapledean had said about the matter. "The ecocatastrophe would have been even worse if it hadn't been for the plague of sterility."

"Maybe," conceded the Dragon Man. "Some said, even then, that we'd have been a lot luckier if the plague had hit a hundred years earlier, in the 1980s instead of the 2030s. If it had, we might have prevented a lot more extinctions. On the other hand, it would have been a lot harder to develop the technologies we needed to save the situation before *we* became extinct. There was no ideal time

137

for any of it to happen. I guess we were lucky to come through it at all."

"Not just lucky," Sara said, seeking further confirmation of the story she'd been told so many times. "Clever and brave."

"Clever and brave," the Dragon Man repeated. "Which, loosely translated, means that when people finally had no choice but to do what was necessary, they did it. Some of them. Enough of them, at any rate. Yes, it needed ingenuity—and yes, it needed heroism. You should feel glad—proud, even—of the fact that the sperm and egg your parents chose to combine as you came out of the old banks, from people whose life histories have been lost. The very fact of their being lost proves that they lived and died in desperate times, heroically...and whether I ever met them or not, I can certainly assure you that if they had known that you would one day be their child, they'd be very, very glad, and very, very proud indeed."

Sara watched the Dragon Man's face very carefully. It had grown familiar by now. In spite of the seeming thinness and hardness of the natural flesh sandwiched between the smartsuit and the skull, the face no longer seemed in the slightest degree unhuman.

There was nothing really new in what the Dragon Man was telling her; she had heard it all from her parents as well as her teachers—but this time, it was coming from the source, from someone who had actually lived through it. Whether Frank Warburton had ever met her biological parents or not, he was of their world; when he spoke for them, he spoke with proper authority.

"Thanks," she said.

"You're welcome," he replied. "About the face...."

"That's not important," she assured him.

"Yes it is," He told her. "It's ugly, and it doesn't need to be. I could use my smartsuit to form a mask indistinguishable from a normal face: a handsome face. Nowadays, somatic engineering gives everyone the opportunity to have a handsome face...and everybody takes the opportunity, except me. There are people older than me, you know, even in Lancashire—but they hide their wrinkles and patches. I don't, even though I know it scares people. I owe you an explanation, if not for scaring you that time in Old Manchester, for pretending just now that there's nothing unusual about me at all."

Sara shook her head. "I'm an apprentice junkie," she said. "Maybe I'll never be a real one, like Father Stephen, but I know what they're doing. They're Preservers of the Heritage of the Lost

World. That's what you're doing—showing the world something lost. I understand."

The Dragon Man stared at her, seeming even more uncomfortable than he had before. "It's not just age," he murmured. "I had a bad accident once...two of them, in fact. The synthetic flesh they used in those days...but you're right. This isn't necessary. You do understand. I'm sorry. Sometimes, I forget just how far the world's evolved while I've been watching it go by...well, thanks for giving me the opportunity to ramble on at you. That shadowbat did me a huge favor—which will add a welcome hint of dramatic irony if it turns out to be one of mine. Let's see, shall we?"

He got up from his own stool and leaned over the bath in which he'd put the rolled-up fabric bearing the secondary trace. He peered at the faint, blurred lines that had appeared in the gel. Then he moved to a desktop whose screen was displaying an image of the surface, and began playing with the keypad. He was only typing with the fingers of his right hand, because his left was gripping the edge of the desk, supporting him in his standing position. He had been moving freely enough when he took the imprints of the shadowbats and set up his equipment, but his body seemed to have stiffened upon while he was perched on the stool. Eventually, he straightened up again.

"Well," he said, after yielding a slight sigh. "I always figured that it would be my fault. No surprise there. See this?"

Sara could indeed see the part of the screen at his finger was pointing, but what it was pointing at she had no idea. She nodded her head anyway.

"It was only a little tweak," he said. "Strictly speaking, the client should have reduced the apparatus he'd already fitted to his suit before adding sublimates to the mix, but you know what teenagers are like—teenagers a few years older than you, that is. They've always wanted more gadgets than synthetic flesh will readily bear. You're sensible enough to take things easy for now, of course. One nice, tasteful rose...but the temptations will come. Boys have to try even harder now than they did in my day. More masks, more hardware, more gimmicks and party tricks. Competition takes different forms, you see."

"I'm sorry," Sara said, plucking up her courage at last, "but I don't have the least idea what you're pointing at."

Mr. Warburton half-turned to look over his shoulder, his expression slightly rueful. "Sorry," he said. "I've been reading proteonomic spectra so long that it's almost like looking at a picture.

139

This trace here"—he tapped the screen with his fingernail—"is probably the fly in the ointment...except that in this case, it's more a case of the ointment in the flyer. I'll have to wait for the proteonome register to put the whole story together, and I probably won't have the tees crossed and the eyes dotted for another four or five hours, but there's enough of a clue here to help me figure out the vague outlines of what must have happened.

"The problem with sublimate organisms, you see—one of the problems, that is—is that they're a trifle oversensitive. They're built to feed on a very limited range of substances secreted by a standard smartsuit. The downside of their ultra-simple diet is that there are a lot of compounds that disagree with them."

"Poisons, you mean?" Sara said, helpfully

"In a way. Let's say that shadowbats have something like an allergy problem. They can lose their shape, or their ability to fly, if they come into intimate contact with the wrong things...which, unfortunately, include some other kinds of suit-fitment. Not roses, or anything that Linda Chatrian deals in, but...do you ever look at the ads on the shopping channels your parents have told you not to watch?"

"Migratory chromocytes," Sara said. "Lepidopteran alate scaling...metaspectral melanin...dermal ivory inlays... those sorts of thing?"

"Those sorts of things," the Dragon Man confirmed, with a wry grin. "Well, I knew that there was a strong possibility of quasi-allergic reactions to one or two of the client's other suit-based systems, so I tweaked a couple of the pseudogenes to strengthen the sublimate's permeability barrier—what wearers would call its smokeskin. I did wonder why the manufacturers hadn't done that themselves, and now I know. The molecular networks that serve to keep bad chemicals out can also operate as traps. When I strengthened the shadowbat's smokeskin so that it would keep more dangerous substances out, I accidentally made it into a sponge for some not-quite-so-dangerous ones...one of which must be a key component of the artificial nectar designed for cosmetic hummingbirds to drink. Do you understand what I mean?"

"I think so," Sara said. "You can never do just one thing—that's the first rule of genetic engineering."

"Exactly. Every planned effect has unplanned side-effects. The nectar wouldn't normally do any harm, but once the shadowbats began soaking it up and concentrating it...well, while we're quoting slogans, you've probably heard the one that says that the poison is the dose. The shadowbats couldn't get rid of the stuff, and it began to disrupt their metabolism. To say that they were getting drunk is probably putting it mildly. Blowing their tiny minds might give a slightly more accurate impression."

"Can you cure it?" Sara asked, looking down at the stricken shadowbat clinging to its shard of flesh.

"I doubt it," the Dragon Man confessed. "The rest of the flock probably didn't make it back to base—which means, I suppose, that you did the right thing to grab one while you could, so I apologize for telling you that you shouldn't have. Their owner probably wouldn't have understood what you meant about one of six even if he had looked at the public noticeboard. I'll contact him this evening, when I can give him a more detailed explanation of what went wrong."

"Will you get into trouble?" Sara asked.

"Perhaps. If the manufacturer wanted to take the matter to court, I suppose my tweaking license could be revoked. I'll have to hope that they take the view that the inherent interest of the finding compensates for the manner in which it was made."

"So I did discover something," Sara said. "It really might be news."

"It's not the kind of news that makes TV, or even the local notice boards, but yes—it's something new, something unexpected, something that might even open up a profitable line of scientific and technological inquiry. If I get any credit, I'll made sure you get credit too, but long experience suggests that the manufacturers will keep all the credit that's going for themselves, as the price of letting me keep my tweaking license...which is hardly fair to you, but nothing either of us can do anything about."

"That's okay," Sara said. "I don't mind, really. I don't want you to lose your license."

The Dragon Man smiled. "Nor do I," he confessed. "Not that I'm likely to need it much longer, of course—but I'm rather attached to it. I've had it well over a hundred years, you know, although I've had to update it three times and only had it modified for sublimates three years ago. I was in business for well over a hundred years before I got it, but I could hardly go back to the kinds of work I was doing in those days. There's no demand for tricks as old as that nowadays."

"They might come back into fashion," Sara suggested, although she was thinking of dragons rather than needles.

"I don't think so," the Dragon Man said, "but I'm not worried. I think I lost my ability to worry a while ago, including my ability to worry about whether the loss of my ability to worry is something I ought to be worried about...and my ability to care much one way or the other seems to have gone with it. I'm still trying to figure out whether it's so hard to give a damn about anything because my emotional spectrum has gone to hell or because there really isn't much worth giving a damn about when you get to my age. Comes to the same thing in the end, I guess."

"Father Lemuel says that it gets harder to feel things as you get older," Sara told him. "He says it's because Internal Technology isn't as messy as the natural systems it has to substitute for. He says we're all turning into robots, although we're doing it so slowly that we don't really notice it."

"Evolution, not revolution," the Dragon Man quoted. "Well, he's only half right. I notice it more and more, nowadays. It gets harder to feel things, and harder to bring back the feelings that go with your memories, but that doesn't prevent you being all too well aware that you aren't the man you used to be. Tell Lem he's too young yet to know what old age really feels like...and with luck, he never will. He's had IT all his life, but I was already old before I got anything more than a few squirts of friendly bacteria. I missed out on being a miracle child, but I'm certainly a miracle now. You have no idea how smart this suit is, or how much help it has from all the deep cyborgery I've taken aboard...but nothing lasts forever, Sara, especially when it's done as much ageing as I have. With luck, you might really be emortal, but I was born too soon. If I thought I had a serious chance to be Achilles' ship I'd be happy to be the guinea-pig, but Achilles' ship didn't have a brain."

"What's Achilles ship?" Sara asked. She had taken note of the fact that the Dragon Man had begun using her first name, but she didn't yet feel able to address him as "Frank".

"An old conundrum," he told her. "Achilles' ship kept going in for repairs. The hull was patched up time and time again, the mast replaced, and then the keel...until there came a time when there wasn't a single one of the original timbers left. Compared to the original, it was a completely new ship—but there was never an identifiable point in time when it had ceased to be the old one. As I said, it's a matter of evolution, not revolution. I've had quite a few replacements myself, and if I thought I could go on living by replacing every bit of natural flesh I had with some ultra-modern synthetic, evolving into a robot, I'd certainly go for it...but my brain can't take

142

that kind of rebuilding, and my body has reached the limits of its tolerance. And if I could go on and on...well, would I still be me, even if I couldn't put my finger on the precise moment that I'd stopped being me?"

Sara frowned in concentration, trying to work out the implications of what the old man was saying. This was the first time she had ever been called upon to ask herself in all seriousness, what might become of her in hundreds of years time.

"But you wouldn't know you'd changed," she said, hesitantly. "You'd still be you, even if it wasn't quite the same you as before. We all change, all the time—but we're always the same person."

The Dragon Man shook his head, although his expression was thoughtful. "I know I've changed," he said, quietly. "I know how much I've changed...and to tell you the truth, Sara, I haven't been quite myself for a while, now. I still remember me...but I sometimes wonder whether there's anything actually left of me but memories."

CHAPTER XX

Sara thought about what the Dragon Man had said for a moment or two, not knowing how to reply. Then she figured it out. "You tweaked the shadowbats," she pointed out. "You're still doing new things."

The Dragon Man smiled again. "And while I can still make mistakes, I can be certain that I'm still alive and as stupid as I ever was," he said. There was a hint of hoarseness in his dry voice, but he sounded more cheerful.

"It's a discovery," Sara reminded him. "Even if we don't get the credit, we did it. You and I."

"And the customer...the boy who wanted the bats fitted, even though his smartsuit was overloaded."

"Him too," Sara agreed. "We can all be glad, and proud."

"I'll certainly try," the Dragon Man promised. "You're right, of course—I was just being melodramatic. My synthetic organs may not have the same capacity for feeling that your real ones do, but I can still be glad, and proud, after my own dull fashion. Lem's right—no matter how hard the techs try to duplicate the emotional orchestra of hormonal rushes and neural harmonies, the music is always slightly out of tune—but that's not the whole story. Not that the way I feel, or don't, is anything I ought to be talking about with a guest, especially a guest as young as you, Sara Lindley. What ought to be exercising our minds, as you correctly observe, is that we've made a discovery. It may not lead to anything, but who can tell?"

"I'm sorry," Sara said, feeling awkward without knowing exactly why. She wondered whether she'd somehow let the Dragon Man down by causing him to say things that he might rather have left unsaid.

"What for?" he said. "You've nothing to be sorry about—and you can tell your parents I said so, if they start on you again when you get home. If you hadn't trapped the shadowbat, we might never have found out what went wrong."

Frank Warburton set all ten of his fingers to the virtual keypad again, and began tapping, presumably making a record of what he had found. Sara couldn't help noticing that the old man's fingers were far less agile than they should have been, given the centuries of practice they'd had.

"I suppose I'd better be getting back," she said, reluctantly. She had not the slightest doubt that her parents would "start on her" again as soon as she got home, and that the Dragon Man's assurance that she'd done the right thing wouldn't be nearly enough to stem the flow of criticism.

"I suppose you had," the Dragon Man agreed—but there was something in his attitude that rang an alarm bell in her head. He hadn't turned to look at her as he'd spoken; his eyes were glued to the screen in front of him. His body, propped against the tabletop, was rigid. Sara knew that it really was time for her to leave, and that her parents would not approve of her having stayed so long, but she couldn't tear herself way from the stool. She watched the Dragon Man typing, hoping to see him relax.

He did relax, but not in a reassuring way. When his body lost its effortful rigidity it sagged against the edge of he bench, as if he couldn't muster the energy to keep it upright any longer.

This time, Sara did pluck up enough courage to say: "Are you all right, Mr. Warburton?"

He stopped typing and turned to look at her, but she wasn't sure whether he had stopped in order to give her his full attention or because his fingers were having difficulty picking out the right keys.

He seemed to be considering the question with all due seriousness, searching for a honest answer.

In the end, he said: "Yes, I am. I'm a little tired—you'd be surprised how tired a man can get, just talking—but the conversation's done me more good than harm. I needed this, I think—the shadowbat, the mystery. Now I need a rest, and you need to pick up a robocab on the other side of the square. I'll see you again, no doubt. Bring Lem, if he'll come. Bring them all—it's about time they started making ready for the twenty-fifth century. Between the two of us, we might just be able to persuade them that the SAPsuit look is one part of our heritage that doesn't need preserving."

While he was speaking, the Dragon Man laid both his palms flat on the bench, to make certain that he couldn't fall. It seemed to Sara that he was almost literally *pulling himself together*.

She relaxed, and said: "It's worth a try. They'll have to respect the wisdom of your years, won't they? Even Father Lemuel."

"I remember when Lemuel was just a boy," the astral tattooist said, forming a broad but slightly lop-sided smile. "And I met Jolene, when she was a little girl younger than you. The others didn't grow up around here, although I met Gus long before your parents got together, and Maryelle too. God, I've been here such a long time—but I don't get out much any more, except for the occasional junk swap. I've become lazy as well as old. Try not to do that, Sara, if you can possibly avoid it."

"Get lazy?" Sara queried, because she genuinely wasn't sure.

"That too," he said, meaning that what he'd really been advising her not to do, if she could avoid it, was to get old.

Sara realized—realizing, too, that this was only the latest in a long string of crucial realizations that she had made during the last few days and hours—that for her, though not for the Dragon Man, getting old really might be a matter of choice, something to be avoided.

"I really will have to go," Sara said, relieved now that it seemed safe to do so. "My parents will be keeping an eye on the clock. I don't want them to worry."

"Me neither," the old man said. "I shouldn't really have asked you to stay, and I shouldn't have rambled on like that, but...well, given that I used up my own child-rearing license a long time ago, I can't help feeling that I'm as entitled as anyone else to take a quasi-paternal interest in other people's. If it takes a village, everyone in the village has a duty to do his part. I'll make sure the shadowbat's reunited with its flock, if that's a possibility. If not...well, let's try to console ourselves with the thought that it didn't die in vain."

Sara stood up, and moved toward the door. The Dragon Man shifted slightly, as if to go before her and open it politely—but the movement seemed painful and it was obvious that he'd be better off resting a while longer.

"It's okay," she said, swiftly. "I can let myself out."

The old man unleashed the longest and deepest sigh that Sara had ever heard, but it wasn't a despairing sound—it was more like a summary of all that had gone before. "I'll square things with the owner and the manufacturer tonight, just as soon as the proteonome analysis has told me the full story," he promised. "Got to be scrupulous now—but I'm glad to have some real work to do, some *real science* to do, and I'll lie down for a while first to make sure I'm up to it. I'll let you know how it all comes out. Thank Lem for me, will you?"

Sara nearly asked what for, but stopped herself just in time. She had worked it out. "I wanted to come myself," she said. "I insisted."

"I know," the Dragon Man replied. "When I was your age, I'd have insisted too."

Sara let herself out of the workroom, and out of the shop. The square wasn't so crowded now—there were only two families staring dutifully at the fire fountain. She stood for a minute watching the multitudinous sparks rise and fall, elements in an endless stream that had been flowing for more than a hundred years, holding its phantom shape as securely as a healthy shadowbat. It was, she realized, a symbol of continuity as well as a pretty display.

She walked unhurriedly across the square, pausing again to let two hummingbirds take turns at her rose. "I've been a bird myself," she murmured to them, "but only in my hood. It's not like real flying. No speed trip at all. Someday, I'll take a look at the world from your angle, and find out what a flower is like in your eyes.

Usually, she thought of getting into a cab for a homeward journey as the end of an excursion. She had been back and forth along the road so many times by now that everything lining it was perfectly familiar—but this time, it didn't seem that her mission of exploration was over yet. This time, she looked out of the cab window with a sense of wonder she hadn't been able to conjure up since her first trip into town eight years before. The world was the same—the liveried cabs, the convoys of trucks, the glittery stone facades, the distant skymasts, the bikers in their finery—but she seemed to be looking at it with new eyes.

"That's the trick of it," she said, aloud. "You just have to keep on finding things out, and the world will always look different, even when it's exactly the same.

"I beg your pardon, miss," the cab's Artificial Intelligence replied, through the microphone mounted in the rear of the driver's "seat". "Do you wish to give me new instructions?"

Maybe I should, Sara thought. *Maybe I should go home the pretty way, if there is one. Maybe I should turn around and head west to the sea, or north to Derwent Water, or east to the windfarms and the SAPorchards. Maybe I should go to see the ruins of London, or the Welsh mountains.*

"No, thank you," she said, aloud. "Just take me home."

"Very good, miss," the cab's AI replied.

"Do you ever get bored?" Sara asked, on a sudden impulse.

"No, miss," the AI assured her. "I am not programmed to experience boredom."

"Nor am I," she informed it. "But it happens anyway. It shouldn't, but it does. How long have you been driving a robocab?"

"This robocab has been in service since January 2364, miss." It wasn't quite what she had asked, but robocabs had a limited conversational repertoire.

"You're a teenager, then—just like me," she said. She got no reply to that at all; the AI obviously had no subroutine set up to deal with comments of that kind. Sara had once thought that all AIs were as clever as adults, but she knew now why Father Gustave and Father Stephen were always calling them "artificial idiots".

"Do you know how long you'll be a robocab driver?" she asked, curiously.

"The current plan calls for the fleet of which this cab is a part to be kept in operation until December 2500, miss," the AI told her. "If, however, there are significant technological advances in the meantime, which outstrip the capacity of its programming, significant aspects of its hardware and software may be replaced."

"You're Achilles' robocab," Sara said. "They'll just keep chipping away, replacing one bit at a time, until you've turned into something else."

"This is not an Achilles robocab, miss," the AI told her. "It is a model 36J1, nicknamed Mercury, owned by the Blackburn Traffic Management Board."

Sara laughed. Robocab AIs weren't programmed to make jokes, either, but that didn't mean that they couldn't play the comedian, with the aid of a sufficiently ingenious straight-person.

"It's been a good day, Mr. Mercury," she told it. "A really good day."

"We aim to please, miss," the cab assured her, as it rolled to a halt at the end of the drive leading to her hometree. "We hope to have the pleasure of your patronage again."

CHAPTER XXI

As soon as Sara stepped across the threshold Mother Maryelle and Father Gustave descended upon her, having obviously laid elaborate plans for further discussion while she'd been out. She assured them that Mr. Warburton had solved the puzzle and had promised to take care of everything. Then she begged to be excused because she still had homework to do and needed to take a shower before the evening meal. As education and cleanliness were things Father Gustave and Mother Maryelle claimed to value very highly, they could hardly refuse.

Almost as soon as Sara was safely in her room, Gennifer called, madly impatient to hear "the whole story" of her adventure in the Dragon Man's lair. It soon became obvious, however, that Gennifer's idea of "the whole story" was rather less extensive than Sara's; Gennifer had only the slightest interest in the underlying cause of the shadowbat's distress, and even less in the Dragon Man's accounts of the Crash, the Aftermath and the paradox of Achilles' ship.

"That's all ancient history," was Gennifer's peremptory verdict. "Whose shadowbats are they? Is it anybody we know? From school, I mean."

Sara had to admit that she didn't know, and hadn't tried very hard to find out.

"You really should get your priorities in order," Gennifer told her. "I'm sure you could have got it out of him if you'd gone about it the right way."

"It's not important," Sara assured her. "Anyway, when the Dragon Man tells him what's happened, he'll probably come looking for me. I'll have to explain why I trapped the shadowbat. I'm sorry, Gen, I really have to do my homework now—dinner will be awkward enough without giving them even more to complain about."

This prophecy proved to be slightly less safe than it seemed. Only three of her parents put in an appearance in the communal dining-room, so Father Gustave, Mother Maryelle and Mother Quilla were able to take turns to lecture her in an unusually orderly fashion. Fortunately, they didn't require any elaborate response from her, so it was a relatively simple matter to let it all wash over her, saving her best line for a parting shot.

"It *was* the right thing to do," she said over her shoulder, as she returned to her room. "Mr. Warburton said so."

"Well, maybe it was," Father Gustave said, lamely, "but you didn't know that at the time, did you?"

Before she went to the bed, Sara made sure that her bedroom window was closed and locked. She set it to display the star-filled skies of night on the dragonworld where she'd taken her maiden flight, but she didn't linger there to watch out for the shadows of flying dragons moving amid the moonlit clouds.

She was still restless, but her Internal Technology helped her to calm her mind. She had descended through all the usual phases of relaxation, and had just lapsed into a peaceful oblivion, when she was summoned back by a peculiar noise.

At first she didn't realize what it was. She wasn't used to hearing sounds in the night, because the hometree's walls were smart enough to deaden the rattle of the wind in its own branches and the sounds of traffic on the road. No soundproof wall could have suppressed this racket, though. Small stones were being hurled at her window, one by one at three-second intervals. The impacts made the plastic fabric reverberate like a sullen drum.

Sara lay dazedly in bed, counting the blows, expecting all the while that the house's resident AI would take whatever action might be necessary to relieve the disturbance. When she had counted seven, though, curiosity took over. She got up, and went to the window.

The dragonworld was perfectly peaceful, but the dragonworld wasn't really there. It only required a single instruction to make the window revert to transparency.

The dazzling flood of unexpected light made her blink furiously, and she had to step back and rub her eyes before she could look out into the garden. The hometree's security lights were on, but the resident AI obviously hadn't yet registered an emergency of sufficient magnitude to warrant waking up her parents. Their windows must all have been tuned to pleasantly dim virtual spaces, so that the glaring light was as invisible to them as it had been to her.

The stone-thrower was shadowed by the garden hedge, and his smartsuit—assuming that it was *his* smartsuit—had been set to mask his face, but it was easy enough to pick out the stones as they soared with uncanny grace from hand to target, disdainful of the property's boundary.

How does he know which window's mine? Sara thought—and then she realized that he must have followed his shadowbats. They had probably evaded his attention on the first night they had made their way to the rose, but on the second occasion he must have kept track of them, reckless of all inconvenience, until the hedge had placed an insurmountable obstacle in his path. There really had been someone there when she had called out into the night—someone who hadn't had the courage to answer her.

He wasn't ignoring the notice I put on the public board because he didn't know that it applied to him, Sara deduced. *He ignored it because he was busy watching over the five that came out, not knowing whether they'd recover if he let them feed and gave them time.*

Because the stone-thrower was standing outside the garden's boundary, he hadn't triggered the kind of trespass alert that might lead to criminal charges, but he was determined to attract her attention. Seen from the outside, awash with the reflected light of the security beams, the window hadn't changed significantly when she'd switched it from picture mode to transparency, so he didn't know that she was standing in the darkened room looking out at him. He continued throwing the little stones, and his aim was remarkably good. He was probably an accomplished sportsman of some kind, although Sara wasn't sure which kind of game would most readily lend its expertise to this kind of expertise.

When Sara's eyes had fully adapted to the light, she was better able to judge the kind of person the shadowbats' owner was. His face and body were hidden, but his throwing arm wasn't, and it was easy enough to judge his height by comparison with the hedge. She guessed that he was probably a couple of years older than she was.

He could have waited till tomorrow, Sara thought.

She opened the window slightly—not enough to risk being hit by a stone, although most of them seemed to be too small to do more than sting her—and called out: "Stop that! You'll wake the whole house!"

"So what?" a barely-broken male voice replied. "You killed my shadowbats, Sara Lindley! Why did you do that? They couldn't do you any harm." He obviously didn't want to wake the whole house, though, because he was speaking just loud enough to be heard—not so loud that the sound couldn't be damped down by the walls protecting her parents' sleep. There was a slight chance that one or two of them might wake up anyway, but the only ones who had windows facing the same direction as Sara's were Father Lemuel and Mother Quilla. Father Lemuel was almost certainly in his cocoon, safe from disturbance by anything short of a clamorous alarm, and Mother Quilla was also a sound sleeper.

"I didn't do anything to your shadowbats," Sara told him. "They did it to themselves. It was an accident. Who are you, anyway?"

"Never mind that, Sara Lindley. I know who *you* are. How did you lure them into your room? What did you do to them once they were in there? They were only supposed to fly around *me*. I want to know what you did to them."

"I didn't do anything," she repeated, irritably. She knew that there was something very odd about what was happening, but she wasn't sufficiently alert as yet to figure out exactly what it was.

"You poisoned my shadowbats, Sara Lindley," he said again. "I'm going to get you for this, Sara Lindley. You'd better watch out. I know who you are, but you don't know who I am."

"Don't be ridiculous," Sara said, trying to cover up her anxiety—although she was more worried about the possibility that the hometree's AI would react to the threat than the much slighter one that he might actually mean it. "Mr. Warburton knows who you are. Mask or no mask, I can find out easily enough. And I didn't poison your shadowbats. They did it themselves. It was Mr. Warburton who tweaked them, but he didn't mean to let them be poisoned. He tweaked them for *your* benefit. It was an unexpected side-effect—an accident, It wasn't anybody's fault. I'm sorry. I didn't want the one I took him to die, but it wasn't me who killed it. Catching it in the jar didn't make any difference."

She'd said far more than she'd initially intended, and she looked around guiltily when she finished, half-expecting to see Mother Quilla standing in the bedroom doorway looking daggers at her. There was no one there; until the hometree's AI decided that there was sufficient reason to wake her parents up, she was safe from interruption...though not, she realized, from the eventual consequences of her actions. All this would be recorded, and it had to be "unusual" enough to be reported to her parents in the morning.

"You caught it in a jar?" the boy said, incredulously. "That's impossible."

"It was sick," Sara said. "I thought it was for the best. I thought it would help the Drag—Mr. Warburton figure out what was wrong. And it did. We figured it out this afternoon. He said he'd call you when he'd finished the job. He should have called you. Didn't he call you?"

"You had no right to catch it," the boy said, although his manner was much more subdued now. "You should have let it come back. It was mine. I should have taken it back to the Dragon Man."

Sara recalled the memory of the shadowbat sinking into the gel that Mr. Warburton had used to take a sample of its molecular make-up, and remembered the way he'd taken an image of the image, and rolled it up...but there was another, more troubling memory lurking behind that one much as the boy was lurking beyond the hedge: the memory of the Dragon Man's lean frame *sagging* when he had momentarily let go of the edge of his desk. He had told her as she left the shop that he was going to lie down for a while before finishing the proteonome analysis and calling his client to pass on the bad news.

"He should have called you by now," Sara said to the boy, anxiously. "He said that he would."

"Well, he didn't," the shadowy figure beyond the garden fence replied. "And it wasn't up to you. It was my shadowbat, and I should have been the one...."

"Shut up!" Sara said, so commandingly that he did. Was it possible, she wondered, that the old man had simply forgotten to call his client? Of course it was—just as it was possible that the proteonome analysis had taken longer than he'd expected. There could be any number of reasons why the Dragon Man hadn't made the call yet. It wasn't urgent. There were any number of reasons why he might have decided to leave it until tomorrow. It was nothing to worry about....

Sara glanced at the wristpad that lay on her bedside table. The luminous time-display was readable even at this distance. Seven hours and ten minutes had elapsed since she had stepped out of the Dragon Man's shop. Perhaps he had yet to complete his analysis. Perhaps he had forgotten his promise to call the owner of the shadowbat...and perhaps not.

"Wait there!" she called to the masked figure. "Don't move!" She realized immediately that he would probably take that as an indication that she was about to call her parents, and thus as a signal to run away as fast as he could, but she hadn't time to worry about that. She turned away from the window, and went to her desktop.

The Dragon Man's phone number was in the machine's ready memory, so she only required a couple of keystrokes to make the call.

When Frank Warburton's remarkable face appeared on the screen, looking considerably fuller and healthier than it had that morning, Sara sighed in relief—but then she realized that the image was a simulation, and that she was dealing with an answerphone AI. "I'm Sara Lindley," she said. "I need to talk to Mr. Warburton in person. It's urgent."

"That's not possible at the present time, miss," the simulation replied, with the typical smoothness of the kind of Artificial Intelligence that was really just an Artificial Idiot.

Sara knew how literal Artificial Intelligences were, and the phrasing sent a chill into her heart. Surely the answerphone ought to have asked her to leave a message, and promised to deliver it as soon as it became convenient. The fact that it hadn't made the promise suggested that it couldn't keep it...but it was only a suggestion

"It *must* be possible," Sara said, although she knew that her insistence was, in this instance, quite impotent. "This is top priority...emergency...red alert...whatever the keyword is. I have to speak to him *now*. I have to."

"That's not possible at the present time, miss," the Dragon Man's image repeated—and this time. Sara allowed herself take aboard the full significance of the statement.

"You mean he's dead, don't you?" she asked, flatly.

The image flickered slightly as a new subroutine kicked in. "I'm sorry, but I can't be reached at present," the sim said, although its pretence to be the person it represented seemed utterly hollow.

"Shit," Sara murmured. She turned on her heel and ran back to the window.

The boy hadn't run away. He was still there, waiting. His posture signaled annoyance and impatience, but he had done what he was told because he was curious to know what was going on.

"Hey, Bat Freak," she called to him, a little louder than was strictly necessary. "How do I get an AI sim to tell me whether or not its master is dead?"

The boy's mouth was already open, poised to utter a complaint, so he had no difficulty at all looking astonished, despite the fact that the rest of his face was obscured by his mask. Five seconds went by before he contrived to speak. "You think the Dragon Man's *dead*?"

he said, too amazed by the inference to object to the form of address she had used.

"How do I get his answerphone to tell me, one way or the other?" Sara demanded.

"You don't," the boy replied, mechanically. "You ask local news. Wow—do you know how *old* that guy was? People like him are rarer than little girls like you—and they aren't making any more of his kind."

Sara didn't bother to react to the "little girl". She had more important matters to attend to, and he was only retaliating to the unflattering form of address she had used. She cursed herself for having been so stupid as to have to ask, but she went back to the desk and called up local news.

There was nothing in the banners, so she typed Frank Warburton's name with an open query. When she read the terse message that came up she didn't know whether to be relieved or not. She went back to the window, because she felt she had to share the news with somebody, and there was only one person readily available who wanted and needed to know.

"He's in the hospital," she told the boy. "He never had a chance to call you. He's comatose. Stable but unconscious."

The boy didn't reply for a few moments. Then he said: "They'll switch him off. Bound to. He's too old. They'll give it a couple of days, then they'll let him go."

"No," Sara said. "He was okay. This morning—this afternoon—he was okay. His brain's fine. It's just a matter...."

Sara trailed off as she heard her bedroom door open. She looked around. Mother Quilla appeared, then Mother Maryelle, but there was nobody else. Obviously, the call to local news had finally tripped the resident AI's alarm, but not at a level of urgency that required the whole house to be woken up. There was obviously some kind of roster, whose existence she had never previously had cause to suspect, determining which of her parents were on call in case of *little* emergencies.

"What's going on?" Mother Quilla demanded.

Sara suppressed the reflex that instructed her to say: "Nothing." She was, after all, no longer a little girl. "It's Frank Warburton, Mother Quilla," she said. "He's been taken to hospital. I was probably the last person who talked to him."

"And you felt compelled to broadcast the news to the empty night, I suppose?" Mother Quilla said—but it was Mother Maryelle who was elbowing Sara out of the way in a conspicuously unmaternal manner so that she could peer out of the window. When Sara glanced back over her shoulder she saw that the boy had vanished from sight, presumably having ducked down behind the fence, but she knew that it would do no good. The hometree had eyes and ears aplenty, although no one ever bothered to interrogate their records unless they had a reason.

"What's his name?" Mother Maryelle demanded, obviously thinking that this was a matter requiring intricate parental negotiations between their two households. "Where does he live?"

"I don't know," Sara muttered, in a forlorn tone. "It really doesn't matter. Not now."

CHAPTER XXII

Because the next day was Monday, Sara had no alternative but to return to her normal routine. She woke up tired and fractious, and breakfast was an unusually somber affair, but when nine o'clock came around she had to be at her desktop with her hood on, logged in to her virtual classroom.

She could tell by the way that the images of the other students looked at her that the news had got around that she'd visited the Dragon Man on Saturday and Sunday, before he'd collapsed at his desk on Sunday evening. The syllabus had its own momentum, though, and Ms. Mapledean couldn't have been less inclined to let anything get in its way if she'd been a tightly-programmed AI—which, since she'd never actually seen her teacher in meatspace, Sara sometimes suspected that she might be.

When the first break came and the school's population was distributed across a new series of virtual spaces, Gennifer suggested that she and Sara should escape into a hidden corner of their own, but Sara refused. She expected to be mobbed by a crowd eager for news, but that wasn't what happened. She was in the main playground, accessible to anyone and everyone, but she found that her classmates were reluctant to flock around her. They seemed to prefer talking about her to talking to her. Gennifer was obviously annoyed with her, but it took some time for Sara to figure out that the others simply didn't know what to say, and were waiting for her to make the first move. Eventually, she went to join Davy Bennett, Julian Sillings, and Margareta Madrovic, whose conversation fell silent as she approached.

"It's all right," she said. "Whatever the Dragon Man has, it isn't catching."

"It wouldn't be catching in virtual space anyway," Davy pointed out, ingenuously.

"Exactly," Sara said. "So why are you avoiding me?"

"We're not," Margareta was quick to say.

"It wasn't my fault he collapsed," Sara said. "He was glad of the chance to have something to do—something to *discover*. He'd have collapsed anyway."

"Nobody thinks it was your fault, Sara," Julian told her. "Has anyone...talked to you about it?"

"The police, you mean? Of course not. So it's all right for you to talk to me about it, if you want to."

"What do you mean, something to *discover*?" Davy wanted to know. Sara didn't know whether or not to be glad that the full story hadn't yet got around. She opened her mouth to start explaining why she had gone to the Dragon Man's shop for a second time, but shut it again when someone else joined the group, approaching from behind so that the first evidence Sara had of his presence was the change in her companions' attitudes. As she turned her head, the slight resistance of the hood's cables provided a sharp reminder of the fact that she was peering into a virtual world at mere simulacrum. She changed stance, so that the newcomer could join the group.

Sara knew immediately who the older boy was—not just his name, but that he must be the shadowbats' owner. She was surprised to find that he seemed shorter than he had the previous night, perhaps because of the angle at which she'd been looking down at him, but that wasn't why she hadn't recognized him.

"Sara Lindley," he said.

"You know I am," she retorted. "Come to get me, have you? Where everyone can watch?"

"Actually," he said, "I came to say sorry. I'm Michael Rawlinson, year eleven."

"I know who you are," she said. "We've met, remember—in the flesh. I was five and you were seven."

He blushed. "I should have realized that you'd have guessed," he said. "Wouldn't take a detective to work out that the likeliest suspect was the boy next door. I should have come right out with it."

"Actually, I hadn't guessed," Sara confessed. "And telling me who you were would have ruined the Masked Avenger act."

"I suppose it would," he conceded. "Afterwards, when I realized that you hadn't poisoned my shadowbats—not deliberately, anyhow...well, here I am, and I'm sorry."

"That's okay," Sara said, putting on a fine show of maturity. "It's really not important. I'm afraid my parents will be in touch with your parents by now, though. I've already run the gauntlet once—your turn is still to come."

"I know," he said. "Shady deals with the Dragon Man...my bats invading a young girl's bedroom...then the Masked Avenger act. When they get their teeth into all of that it'll be the most fun they've had since I crashed a glider into the best greenhouse. Only a little one, mind—not the kind you actually sit in. Now I can tell them that I've apologized to you, that might help cut the barrage short, maybe by as much as an hour."

"Is that why you did it?" Sara asked.

"No, I really am sorry. I jumped to the wrong conclusion. It was stupid."

"In that case," Sara said, glad to have the opportunity to take the moral high ground, "you can tell your parents I forgive you. In your place. I'd probably have jumped to the wrong conclusion too. If something had happened to my rose...."

"It's a nice rose," Michael Rawlinson told her. "I couldn't really see it last night, but I clicked on your tag just now to get the picture. It really suits you."

If he'd phrased the compliment slightly differently, Sara might have been delighted by it—and astonished by its source—but it echoed far too closely the first words the Dragon Man had ever spoken to her. She felt tears welling up in her eyes, and felt profoundly grateful that she was wearing a hood instead of sitting in front of her desktop camera. All that the older boy and her three classmates could see was a synthesized image of her face; they knew which way she was looking, but they couldn't see the tears. The hood was sensitive to her expression, though, and it was feeding that emotional intelligence to the program synthesizing her appearance.

"Are you all right?" asked Julian Sillings.

"Of course she's all right," Michael Rawlinson said, snappishly.

"Why did she call you the Masked Avenger?" Davy Bennett inquired, obviously feeling that Julian's question had opened up the conversation to anyone who cared to join in.

"None of your business," the older boy retorted, glaring at Davy before turning back to Sara. "Are you all right?" he asked, in a very different tone.

"Of course I'm all right," she said, having recovered her composure. "You said so yourself, didn't you?"

"Yes I did," he agreed, as if that were absolute proof. "Anyway, I just wanted to say I'm sorry. I can call you if you like, to let you know how the thing with my parents works out."

Sara almost said "Why would I want to know?" but she stopped herself just in time, partly because she caught a glimpse of the expression on Margareta's face. She swallowed the intention, and waited until she was sure that she could form the words clearly before saying: "Yes—do that. We might have to compare notes to figure out how to get both lots off our backs."

"Right," Michael Rawlinson said, before floating away in an elegant, rather dreamlike fashion that real space would never have tolerated.

"It's the rose," Sara told Margareta, airily. "You ought to think about getting one yourself.

"What was all that about?" Davy wanted to know—but the time available for explanations was already gone, and they all had to return to the classroom for a dose of Mid-level Multiversal Navigation.

The story came out anyway, as it was bound to do, in dribs and drabs. Sara only had to tell her side of the story once, and leave the grapevine to take care of its dissemination. She was careful, though, not to make Mike Rawlinson's actions seem unreasonable—and she hoped that he would do likewise. By the time the school day was concluded, everyone in the school must have heard about what had happened to Mike's shadowbats, and what the Dragon Man had found out about them, and at least some rumor of what had taken place on either side of the Lindley household's garden fence in the small hours.

When Sara finally put the hood aside for the last time there was an almost immediate knock at her door. She guessed that the resident AI had been commanded to notify her parents—or one of them, at least—that she was free. She was expecting one of her Mothers, but it was actually Father Lemuel. He came in and sat down in her armchair, leaving her to remain perched on the swivel-chair at the desk.

"I tried to see Frank," he told her. "Not possible. Stupid, isn't it? I haven't seen him for...I don't know, twenty years at least, and never even realized we were out of touch. Now...." He didn't attempt to finish the sentence.

"He's going to die." Sara said.

Father Lemuel eyed her warily. "Yes," he said. "I'm afraid he is."

"He knew that," Sara said. "He as good as told me, only I wasn't quick enough on the uptake. Not that he expected it as soon as last night—but soon enough. He asked me to give you his regards, and to thank you."

"For what?"

"For letting me take the shadowbat to him. For not taking over."

"I only paid the cab fare," Father Lemuel told her. "You were the one who insisted."

"You know what I mean," she told him. "Mike said they'd be bound to switch him off. Do you know when they'll do it?"

"Mike?" Father Lemuel queried.

"Rawlinson. Hasn't Father Aubrey contacted the chairperson of his parental committee yet?"

"Oh, that Mike," Father Lemuel said, with a faint grin. "You know, Sara, there's only one thing in the world worse than a meeting of eight disgruntled parents, and that's a meeting of two sets of eight disgruntled parents. I'd give anything to miss that one, but I suppose I have to put in an appearance."

"If you didn't," Sara pointed out, "our side would be outnumbered. When will they do it, Father Lemuel—turn Mr. Warburton's life-support off, I mean."

"I don't know," Father Lemuel told her. "They'll want to make sure that they've explored every possibility. Dying's such a rare event these days that the doctors are reluctant to let anyone go—even people as old as Frank."

"They can't replace his brain," Sara told him. "He told me that. Did he ever mention Achilles' ship to you?"

Father Lemuel shook his had, but said: "I know the story, though. Actually, his brain's in good shape, all things considered. Twenty-second-century neuronal renewal technologies might have been primitive by today's standards, but Frank always had a good brain—never a trace of senility. It was his body let him down, then and now. A person isn't just a brain, you know—even leaving the brain out of it, you can't just keep switching bits of body like the spars and rigging of Achilles' ship. A whole person is a lot more than the sum of his parts."

"He tried to explain that to me," Sara admitted. "He couldn't quite find words that he was sure I'd understand."

"I know the problem," Father Lemuel said. "I'm only a hundred and forty-nine, but it still seems a long time since I was a child. Modern parenting requires us to build some strange and difficult bridges."

"I think I understand, though," Sara said. "He was glad to have the chance to do one more thing, solve one last puzzle...."

"Slay one last dragon," Father Lemuel supplied.

"No," Sara said. "He was a dragon-maker, not a dragon-slayer."

"Right," said Father Lemuel, accepting the correction. "He was an artist. Nobody ever reckoned him a great artist, because he was content to stay in his own corner doing his own thing for year after year after year, never clamoring for attention or attracting much...but no one who didn't live through the Crash and the Aftermath has any right to criticize a man who knew the real value of simply being alive. There's no one else like him you know. There are older people, even in Lancashire—maybe hundreds in the country, tens of thousands in the world—but they'll all be gone soon enough, and every one of them is unique. They're all dragon people, in a way: fabulous creatures, born on one side of an Age of Ruin and dying on the other. When all his kind are gone there'll be no one left who knows what it was really like to live in the old world, no matter how many assiduous collectors of pre-Crash junk there are, or how many expert historians."

Sara realized that Father Lemuel hadn't come to see her just for her benefit, but for his too. He wanted to talk, not just to anyone, but to her. She remembered what he'd said about strange and difficult bridges—but among the many things she was now beginning to understand was a sense of the fact that all of her parents sometimes found it a great deal easier to talk to her than to talk to one another. Even Frank Warburton, who had only met her properly the day before, after seeing her once at a junk swap in Old Manchester and being afraid that his horrid face might have frightened her, had found it easier to talk to her on his last day of consciousness than it would have been to talk to Father Lemuel, or any other adult.

What must the world have been like, she wondered, when children were so common that two parents might have five or six of them, and never want for anyone to talk to?

"I'm glad I went to see him," Sara said. "In a way, it makes it more painful to know that he's dying—but that's better than it being...irrelevant."

"Yes it is," Father Lemuel said. "I'm glad you went to see him too. Because I didn't, you see. In a way, that makes it more painful that he's dying too—but it's better by far than it being irrelevant. Imagine living in the old world, when death was commonplace!"

Sara started slightly at that perverted echo of her own thought, but she knew it was just a coincidence. "Will I be allowed to go to the funeral?" she asked.

"We all will," Father Lemuel told her. "I don't know who his executor is, but given the circumstances, I suspect that you'll be offered a good seat, if you want it."

"I'd like that," Sara said. "I'd like it even better if he regained consciousness and went back to work, though, if only for a little while."

"So would we all," Father Lemuel agreed.

CHAPTER XXIII

As things turned out, it took ten days for the county hospital's Ethics Committee to agree with representatives of the Neuroanalytical Unit that Frank Warburton's body and brain were no longer able to work together in such a way as to maintain his personality, no matter how many neuronal reconnections the surgical team's nanobots might contrive to restore and renew. He was "released" within the hour.

Sara understood well enough what the word "released" signified when her desktop messaging system, obedient to its programming, broke into the middle of a history lesson to whisper the news in her ear. It meant that the machines maintaining the semblance of life within the old man's faded flesh had been stood down to await more profitable duties.

Sara had already learned from publicly accessible records that Frank Warburton was—had been—two hundred and eighty-two years, nine months, and fourteen days old. It wasn't a record, even for the county, let alone the country, but there weren't many people of that age who were hard at work when their consciousness was eclipsed for the last time. There had, it seemed, been no other who had clung to what was effectively the same profession since his twenty-first century teens, in spite of at least half a dozen transformative technological revolutions. That small element of uniqueness enabled the report to make the national news, carefully colored by the uniquely respectful kind of melodrama that was typical of modern obituaries.

According to the text Sara read in the national broadcast, Frank Warburton had collapsed "while conscientiously analyzing a mistake that he had made as a result of his overadventurousness in trying to meet the requests of a client who was too young to have sufficient credit to have the job done properly." Apparently, the item went on to explain, Frank Warburton had always been willing to innovate, especially on behalf of the young. This particular mistake, the newswriter noted, had thrown up some interesting information regarding previously-unnoticed possibilities inherent in sublimation technology, which might increase the utilitarian potential of "shaped sublimates" considerably. The funeral would be on the fourteenth of September

Sara's name was not mentioned in connection with the "interesting information"; nor was anyone else's.

"That's so unfair," Gennifer told her, when the day's school was finally over and they were able to go on-camera for an intimate exchange of views. "You were the one who made the discovery, not him. They're only making him out to be a hero because he's dead. If he were still alive they'd have called him an irresponsible tamperer and taken away his license."

"Which would probably have killed him," Sara said, not being at all certain that it hadn't been exactly that prospect that had tipped him over the edge. "He deserves all the credit. He did the tweaking, and he figured out what it was that he'd done. Anyway, responsible people who only do what they're supposed to do, like our faithful family tailor, never discover anything. It's the people who don't follow the instructions who make progress."

"Very big of you," Gennifer said. "Personally, I'd have made a fuss. You might not be entitled to any royalties, but you could have made the national news."

"The quiet kind of celebrity that children already have," Sara informed her, oozing mature sophistication, "is more substantial, in its way, than anything brokered by TV." But Gennifer didn't understand what she meant.

"Are you going to the funeral?" Gennifer asked. "They say it's going to be big. A man that age knows a lot of people—my Mother Leanne says that she and Father Jacob both met him, although Father Jacob claims to have forgotten all about it. I wish my parents would take me, but they won't. You and I will still have to wait for Christmas for our first meeting in meatspace."

"Yes," Sara said, when she was finally able to get a word in. "I am going. I'll be in the Hall, in fact."

Gennifer was impressed. "How did your parents wangle that?"

"They didn't," Sara said, proudly. "I might not have made the national news, but I was a witness to his last hours—that's how the executor put it. When I say I'll be in the Hall, that's what I mean. Just me. Not even Father Lemuel, although he's known the Dragon

Man for more than a century, off and on, and he's determined to be in the memorial garden in the flesh even though he's practically a cocoon-addict nowadays."

Gennifer was now beyond being impressed; she was awestruck. "My God!" she said. "Imagine how many women wearing hummingbirds there'll be at a do like that! Thousands!"

"They won't be allowed to fly in the Hall," Sara reminded her. "There's such a thing as decorum. In fact, they won't be flying in the memorial garden either. It says so on the invitation, in so many words. All mobile accessories must remain fixed for one hour after the revelation of the memorial stone."

"Why?" Gennifer asked.

"Decorum," Sara repeated, with all the dignity she could muster. "It's a funeral, not an eight-way marriage or a naming day." Even as she said it, though, she remembered seeing funeral ceremonies on the TV in which the memorial gardens had been filled with flocks of colored birds, which couldn't possibly have been natural. Perhaps, she thought, the Dragon Man had left special instructions.

"Lucky you had that rose fitted, isn't it?" Gennifer observed.

"Is it?" Sara said. "He's dead, Gen. I don't call that lucky."

"He'd have died anyway. This way, you get a front seat at a really big funeral. You didn't kill him, you know. It wasn't your fault he was working on a Sunday evening, and even if he'd been cozily cocooned in his bedroom he'd still have pegged out on the Monday."

"It's still not lucky," Sara insisted. "It's just not the right word. Father Gustave says that it's been good for me to make the intimate acquaintance of death, but that's not right either. It's not luck, and it's not good. It's...well, I don't know what it is, but there is such a thing as decorum."

"So you keep saying. Well, I envy you. Will Mike Rawlinson be there, do you think? It was his shadowbat, after all."

"I don't know," Sara said. "I haven't had a chance to talk to him today. I'll call him later if he doesn't call me first."

"Will you, now? Maybe you'll be going to stay with *him* for Christmas."

"He only lives just down the road," Sara reminded her. "I can walk to his hometree as easily as he can walk to mine. This whole thing wouldn't have happened otherwise. We don't need to fix up formal visits."

"He's two years older than you are," Gennifer pointed out, cattily. "You're not old enough to be his best friend.

166

"In the great scheme of things, two years is nothing," Sara told her. In a hundred years time, our ages will be closer than the ages of any two of my parents, or his...or yours, for that matter."

"Oh, be like that," Gennifer said. "Anyway, I won't say enjoy yourself at the funeral, given that you've come over so sensitive, but you still have to tell me the whole story, in more detail than you tell it to anyone else, okay? We're sisters, remember—or as close as anyone ever gets to being sisters nowadays, or ever will again."

"Sisters," Sara repeated, glad to find that the word sounded appropriate.

Gennifer was right, Sara thought; now that all children were born in artificial wombs, from eggs and sperm dutifully deposited in the bank by parents who's been far too polite to exercise their right of replacement while they were still alive, it was unlikely that earthbound humankind would ever again produce any biological sisters, although things were different in the Lagrange colonies. If the earthbound ever did produce any more biological sisters, it was unlikely in the extreme that the sisters in question would be alive at the same time—but that only meant that the word "sister" had been liberated, as the word "junkie" had been, and was now free to acquire new meanings. Yes, she and Gennifer *were* sisters, in a brand new sense that made the fact all the more remarkable and all the more exciting. "I'll tell you everything," she added, when Gennifer made no further response. "Everything."

As soon as she had broken the link, she called Mike Rawlinson. "You heard the news?" she said.

"Yes," he said. "I got a whisper during history. I wanted to come and talk to you, but I had things on—commitments I couldn't break. My parents have been bending my ear ever since I logged off. I've only just only escaped. Same with you?"

"No," Sara said. "Either they're being diplomatic and leaving it up to me to mention it first, or they've said everything that had to say already. The last ten days has been a long time. Are you going to the funeral?"

"Yes, of course. I'll see you in the memorial gardens—but I'll have my parents with me, so it'll just be a matter of waving hello and goodbye."

"I'll be in the Hall for the eulogies," Sara told him, not in the least triumphantly.

"That's fair," he said. "You were the last person to see him. If you'd stayed a little longer you'd probably have seen him collapse."

"He didn't want that," Sara told him. "I couldn't have done anything. His IT was rigged to send out an immediate distress call—the ambulance wouldn't have got to him any sooner."

"I know," Mike assured her. "I only meant that it's right that you should be in the Hall. I'll still see you in the gardens afterwards. I wish I still had the shadowbats—the manufacturers offered me another flock, but I said no. It wouldn't have seemed right."

"I'd quite like to have something to remember him by," Sara said. "Nothing big—a little figure of some kind, on my arm or shoulder. Just a picture, not a flyer or one of Davy's creepy spiders. A golden dragon, like the one in his window."

"It's not there any more," Mike told her. "The shop's been cleared out. It's up for sale. I don't know what happened to all his stock, or his archives. My Father Benjamin says that he must have had a massive archive, but I'm not so sure he was the kind of man to keep all his old stuff in drawers and cupboards."

"I saw him at a junk swap once," Sara said. "He collected old tattooing equipment."

"That's different. Anyway, it's all gone, whatever there was. His executor will probably sell it off. Do you know his executor? Someone called Janis Leggett, apparently."

"She lives on the south coast, in Hove," Sara told him, having looked the woman up. "She's his daughter."

"His biological daughter?"

"He wasn't *that* old. He was a natural born himself, but he was a parent like our parents. She's like me—the product of an anonymously-donated egg from the early days of the great plague. I'll be interested to meet her."

"Is she a sublimate technologist too?" Mike wanted to know.

"No. She's an oceanographer in the UN's Climate Bureau. Must have followed in the footsteps of one of her other parents, unless she struck out on her own."

"I might do that," Mike said. "Oceanography, that is, not strike out on my own. My Mother Gaea's a marine ecologist."

"You have a mother called Gaea?" Sara asked. "I bet Father Stephen and Father Aubrey made up some nice jokes about that after the big joint meeting. I'm surprised they haven't told them all to me."

"It's not an uncommon name," Mike said, a little stiffly. "Anyway, the jokers in my family had some fun with Lemuel. We're lucky that kind of thing's gone out of fashion. What do *you* want to do when you grow up?"

"Lots of things," Sara told him. "There'll be time enough to try all sorts of work, on Earth and off it. Someday, I'll go to the moon. By then, who knows what further horizons there'll be?"

"Which of your parents said that to you?"

"All of them, at one time or another. Haven't yours?"

"They're more a *don't-rush-into-things-and-don't-try-to-run-before-you-can-walk* sort of crowd. It's a wonder they ever got around to applying for a license at all, let alone with one another. Did you ever hear the one about a camel being a horse designed by a parental house-meeting?"

"Camels were extinct before parental house-meetings started," Sara pointed out. "I believe the original reference was to committees in general."

"Well," Mike said, theatrically, "they'd have been extinct a long quicker if my parents had been the committee in question, if they'd ever got off the drawing board in the first place. I bet Janis Leggett's parents could have done a much better job—they had the Dragon Man. He wouldn't have been content with a horse, though. He'd have given it wings, and a horn on its forehead too."

"Yes he would," Sara agreed. "There'll never be anyone like him again. Never. And no matter how long people like Father Lemuel may have known him, we'll be the ones who remember him longest—you and I. We were part of his last adventure."

The older boy smiled at that, but not condescendingly. He smiled to show that he knew what she meant, and felt the same way. "See you at the funeral, Stinky Rose," he said.

"You too, Bat Freak," she replied.

CHAPTER XXIV

The indoor funeral ceremony was rather tedious, in Sara's opinion. It might have been more interesting if the information about Frank Warburton contained in the various eulogies had been new to her, but by the time the big day came she'd been trawling the web for days and she probably knew more about the man than any mere human acquaintance could possibly remember. The eulogists had undoubtedly consulted the same sources, but propriety demanded that they pretend to be speaking from memory as well as from the heart, so the word-pictures they painted were as hazy as shadowbats in the dusk.

Janis Leggett was, alas, no exception. More than a hundred years had passed since Frank Warburton had been one of her adoptive parents, but Sara had always been assured by her own Mothers and Fathers that although the collective household would not remain together for more than twenty years or so, they would remain her parents forever. Although Sara had never given the matter intensive thought, she had assumed that she would remain in contact with all her parents, and that she would probably draw closer to them as individuals once she no longer had to confront them as a barely-organized mob on a daily basis.

The Dragon Man's daughter, by contrast, freely confessed that she had not seen Father Frank in the flesh for seventy years, and only ever talked to him on the phone when he called her. She made what was obviously intended to be a humorous reference to his ineptitude in calculating time differences when he called her in the South Atlantic—supplemented by a joke about the time-zone difficulties the UN would face if it really did relocate to the south pole—but Sara could see nothing funny in the fact that Frank Warburton had had to try so hard to obtain the attention of his daughter that he had chosen to ignore his desktop AI whenever it told him that she was likely to be fast asleep, because she was somewhere so distant from him that she was living ten or eleven hours ahead of him.

In spite of her determination to remain focused on the speakers, Sara found her attention wandering. She never went so far as to stop thinking about the man whose absence her presence was supposed to be honoring, but she did take leave to wonder how much of his work was on display in the solemn crowd.

There were, as Gennifer had prophesied, an inordinate number of hummingbirds among the living jewelry on display. They were not merely perched on dozens of shoulders like fancy epaulettes but clustered around dozens of elaborate head-dresses and occasionally distributed about in meticulously-linked flocks around the billowing sleeves and pleats of the most ostentatious costumes Sara had ever seen in meatspace. None of these, Sara felt sure, were Frank Warburton's work. In his youth, when "tattoos" really had been tattoos, his work might have seemed garish to some—especially when he inscribed brightly-colored dragons in the real flesh of people's upper arms, torsos and ankles—but by today's standards a sublimate engineer was a subtle artist, whose works were exceptionally discreet.

Sara remembered the tone of the Dragon Man's voice as he had told her that sublimate accessories didn't have to be shadows—that they could be as bright as angels or as subtle as phantoms. She had not thought about it much at the time, but she was convinced, now, that he must have been nursing plans for designs far more subtle than any that had yet been advertised. In the meantime, he had fitted Davy's spiders and Mike's bats, glad to help out with their adolescent pretences—but his ambitions, Sara knew, had far exceeded the scope that had yet been granted to him. He had been waiting patiently for the slow wave of fashion to move beyond gimmickry and frippery, and for the potential of the new technology to unwind into a spectrum of splendid opportunity. Alas, he had not had the time to wait.

Unlike the females in the audience—all but a few of whose personal embellishments made Sara's purple rose seem modest in the extreme—the males had set their smartsuits to black, mimicking the formal mourning-dress of the Lost World rather than more recently obsolete SAPsuits. Even if a few shadowy sublimates had been allowed to cling to such costumes—while brighter angels and diaphanous ghosts were hidden away, along with the more substantial produce of former fashion-eras—they were quite invisible.

There was not a dragon to be seen anywhere in the room, and certainly nothing flamboyantly pictorial, in the vein of Washington

171

crossing the Delaware. Not one of her parents had been able to interpret that particular joke for Sara, but the phrase was sufficiently exotic not to call up too many hits on a search engine when fed in as a unit; there was even a pre-Crash audio file available, whose survival of the centuries was even more remarkable than Frank Warburton's. Sara suppressed the irreverent tune as it rose unbidden into her memory, and concentrated harder on the present speaker, who had been introduced as the president of some sort of trade union of sublimate engineers. So far as Sara could tell, he had never even met Frank Warburton, although he did seem to be speaking with genuine appreciation about his work—not just his astral tattoos but all his work, including the golden dragon in his window.

It would have been nice, Sara thought, if the image of that dragon, which had hung for so many years in Mr. Warburton's shop window, had been mounted on the wall behind the speaker's podium. She had no idea what had happened to it; as Mike Rawlinson had told her, the shop had been stripped bare and no one seemed to know what had become of its fittings.

"It should be here," Sara murmured, not meaning to speak aloud. She blushed as she realized that she had translated the insistent thought into an audible whisper, but calmed herself when she decided that it had been too quiet for anyone else to hear—not even Linda Chatrian, who was sitting beside her, having promised her parents to "keep an eye on her".

It should be here, Sara repeated to herself, more discreetly. *He should be here, but he's not.*

Sara savored the layers of meaning contained in the two observations. Frank Warburton was indeed, not here; that was why the funeral was taking place. But he was not present, either, in the eulogies that were being offered, turn and turn about, by people who had known him well a hundred or two hundred years before or had some slight acquaintance with his current work. Nor was he present in the hundreds of smartsuits gathered in the Hall to which he might have made some small decorative contribution. It was as if he had been buried—not literally, even though he was the product of an era when the dead sometimes had been buried—but buried in the minds of his closest friends beneath murky layers of forgetfulness, and buried in the second skins of all his myriad clients by stubborn strata of fashion and convention.

Sara felt a new significance in the fact that she had been "a witness to his last hours". She felt, in fact, that, by virtue of that freak of chance, she had come as close to the real Frank Warburton—as close, that is, to the person he had been at the moment of his death—as anyone in the world.

She had looked around for Mike Rawlinson before she entered the Hall of Remembrance, but she had not found him in the slowly-gathering crowd that was assembling in the Memorial Garden to watch the ceremony on the hall's exterior display-screen. It seemed to her unjust that Linda Chatrian was sitting beside her rather than him. Mike had, after all, been the catalyst that had brought her together with the Dragon Man, thus allowing her to form a unique bond with him, quite unlike any she had formed with her various parents. Mike was the one who had been moved by grief and wrath to trek across country for a whole kilometer to confront her at the window through which his Gothic emblems had been mistakenly lured. He, too, was not here.

And the eulogists droned on.

"This is pointless," Sara murmured. Again she spoke the words aloud, but too quietly to be overheard—or so she thought, until Linda Chatrian said "Sssh!" loudly enough for at least half a dozen of their neighbors to hear.

Sara blushed, and bit her tongue.

After that, she hardly dared to form a coherent sentence in the privacy of her own thoughts, for fear that it might escape and attract the censorious attention of the whole crowd. Fortunately, the eulogies had not much further to run, and the indoor part of the ceremony was concluded soon enough.

It seemed to take forever for the crowd to file out through the doors of the Hall of Remembrance. The weight of the occasion made every step ponderous, and provoked an excessive politeness whenever two people came into competition to occupy the same space—with the result that spaces which could have been put to perfectly good use often went begging for thirty or forty seconds, until someone finally accepted the necessity of moving ahead of whoever was gesturing them forward with ever-increasing urgency.

Sara was one of the last to leave, although Ms. Chatrian made an ostentatious display of ushering her out in advance of her own venerable presence.

Ms. Chatrian was wearing neither flowers nor avian jewelry, although she had not gone so far as to manifest herself in masculine black. She was clad in all the colors of precious metal, from platinum white through gold to burnished copper—all of which seemed to melt as she moved.

While she was a child, Sara had never thought of Ms. Chatrian as anything less than the perfect embodiment of grace, deportment and fashionability, but she was close enough now to detect a certain stiffness of limb and awkwardness of gait that had to be symptoms of ageing, and it was all too obvious that the tailor's sense of what was in vogue really had fallen behind the times. Sara knew now, because she had checked, that Linda Chatrian was more than two hundred years old—considerably older than any of her parents.

Sara had rejoined her Mothers and Fathers before she finally caught sight of Mike Rawlinson, who was similarly surrounded by his family. Although the two families had met up *en masse* in virtual space to discuss the stone-throwing incident, they were ostentatiously ignoring one another now—but that calculated ignorance extended as far as giving no sign that anyone in either party noticed the greetings that their children pantomimed to one another.

Ten days earlier, the fact that Sara was able to meet the eyes of an older boy so forthrightly, and exchange conspiratorial grimaces with him, would have seemed highly significant, if not utterly amazing. Now, though, it seemed entirely natural.

There were a dozen other boys close enough not to be obscured by the crowd, whose ages ranged from about twelve to seventeen. Sara knew that every one of them was aware of her presence, and that every single one of them would look longer and harder at her than at any of the other girls within *their* sight. Ten days earlier, that knowledge would have terrified her—but not now.

"How was the ceremony, Sara?" whispered Mother Verena. As well as the fixed screen on the outer wall of the Hall there was another on the top of the hill on which the memorial stones were ranked, so everyone in the larger crowd must have been able to see the eulogists in close-up and hear every word they had to say—but Sara knew that Mother Verena hadn't asked the question because she wanted to know what had happened. She had asked the question because she wanted to give Sara the opportunity to give voice to her feelings.

"It was very moving," Sara lied, as she felt obliged to do.

Linda Chatrian was still close enough to favor her with a sharp glance, but the tailor said nothing—as she, in her turn, doubtless felt obliged to do.

"They're about to unveil the stone," said Father Gustave. "What took you so long?"

"No they're not," said Father Lemuel. "It'll take another ten minutes for all the people from the Hall to get into position."

"The stewards are having a terrible time trying to distribute the newcomers," Father Aubrey observed.

"I can't think why they're being so fussy," Mother Quilla said. "Why does everything have to be just so?"

"It's because they're men," Mother Jolene said. "Old men. Very hierarchical. Everyone wants the exact spot that was allocated to him. Men at the top of the hill, women at the bottom. The trouble with living so long is that attitudes no longer change at the same pace as technology."

"They never did, Jo," said Father Lemuel.

"Well, Lem, the gap's getting wider every day," Mother Jolene came back. "Let that be a lesson to you, Sara. You may be living in the twenty-fourth century, but all those old fogies elbowing one another out of the way on the crest of the hill will never get out of the twenty-first, even if they manage to live till the next double-zero year."

Sara followed the direction of Mother Jolene's disapproving gaze with her own eyes, to the place where a company of "old fogies" really did seem to be jockeying for position with undue haste and force. She recognized the president of the sublimate engineers' trade association, who seemed to be trying to restore order. Fortunately, he seemed to be succeeding. Everyone lining the ridge of the sloping garden now seemed to be arranged, more or less, in some sort of pre-planned formation.

"They're not all old," Father Stephen pointed out, punctiliously.

"They are all men, though," Mother Maryelle put in, as if she'd only just noticed.

"Not all," said Mother Quilla, ever avid to match Father Stephen in pedantry. "Just because they're almost all wearing black, it doesn't mean that...."

Mother Quilla stopped in mid-sentence, partly because of the shock and partly because her pedantic judgment had just been overtaken by events.

Sara blinked in surprise, and drew in her breath sharply.

The people gathered in orderly ranks at the top of the hill were no longer wearing black—not all of them, at any rate. They had activated metamorphic transformations preprogrammed into their smartsuits, and they were undergoing a spectacular collective transformation.

It would have been even more spectacular, Sara judged, if they had coordinated their timing a little better, but they were too many for that, and there still seemed to be a certain residual confusion about exactly who was supposed to be positioned exactly where.

Father Lemuel's estimate proved, in the end, to be conservative. Even though it had now become obvious that something was afoot, the minutes dragged on and on as the people making ready continued to make ready, presumably chiding one another for inept timing as rudely as they had earlier demanded more space.

Some little time before the display progressed to its next phase, Sara had worked out what was going to happen—but that only made waiting for it all the more testing. She understood now why the invitations had specified that all detachable decorations were to remain attached for an hour after the revelation of the memorial stone.

At the moment when the stone was finally revealed, Frank Warburton's work took to the air.

CHAPTER XXV

Because a little of Mother Quilla's and Father Stephen's pedantry had rubbed off on her, Sara knew that it couldn't really be all of Frank Warburton's work that was taking to the air, because sublimate accessories had only been a part of his most recent endeavors. She knew, too, that most of the accessories he'd actually fitted to his customers' smartsuits had been things of no great distinction—which meant that only the tiniest fraction of this display could actually have consisted of creatures he'd made and supplied. But this was neither a duplication of nor a tribute to his mundane accomplishments.

It was a mirror of his dreams.

Sara knew that by far the greater part of what survived of the Dragon Man's everyday labours was bound into the real and artificial flesh of his customers, many of whom were long dead, and other miscellaneous living canvases, many of which were long discarded. Most of his accomplishments were lost in the infinite obscurity of the past. What remained was doubtless spectacular, but this was far more than a remainder.

There were shadowbats by the thousand. Most of them were tiny, but some of were them so large that they could have folded themselves around a living person—even an athlete—like a cloak. Some of them were huger still, unwearable by anyone but a giant, designed as if for human beings who were yet to be, but in reality not for human beings at all. These were shadowbats whose only reason for existence was to *be* shadowbats, not accessories to other beings' lives and costumes.

There were shadowbirds and shadowbees, and shadow beings that were no mere mimics, but potential inhabitants of whole shadow worlds—not virtual worlds contained within the illusory glass of picture windows, but worlds in real space, like the islands where genetic engineers were trying to recreate all the species lost to extinction during the Crash, or the planets of alien suns which no interstellar probe had yet contrived to reach.

There were creatures made of fire—fiery flies and fiery birds and fiery serpents—which reminded Sara of something Ms. Mapledean had one told her class about life being a process of slow combustion, in which the body burned the food it took in as fuel, not merely to provide the energy of movement but the energy of thought and the energy of imagination.

There were other bright creatures too, like the angels of which Frank Warburton had spoken, entities not of living fire but of a purer living light.

There were UFOs.

There were Chinese kites.

There were flying fish and flying flowers.

There were even flying pigs.

The display was neither solemn nor entirely serious. It was playful and exuberant. It was hectic, as if with irrepressible laughter.

Suddenly, the jostling of the "old fogies" on the hilltop no longer seemed silly or irreverent. Only a few of them had ever met Frank Warburton, or had even been familiar with his work, but they had been his colleagues, his peers, his fellow tinkerers, his fellow adventurers. They had been the people capable of giving form to the dreams that he had entertained, but to which he had not yet been able to give form himself. They were the people capable of constructing his real memorial, and they had not merely been willing to do that but eager to do it.

There was a sense, Sara knew, in which they were advertising themselves and their profession. There was a sense in which this was all publicity, calculated to generate commercial gain. But that didn't mean that it wasn't a fitting celebration of Frank Warburton's life and career. That didn't mean that it wasn't an appropriate tribute to Frank Warburton's long survival and still-unfulfilled ambitions.

There were dragons, too.

Most of all—because they were so large, so imperious and so magnificent, and because Frank Warburton had, after all, been a Dragon Man among Dragon Men—there were dragons.

Some were red and some were gold. Some were royal blue and some were imperial purple. Some were every color under the sun, not to mention quite a few that defied the sun to illuminate their mystery.

Oh yes, there were dragons a-plenty.

The most remarkable thing of all, however, was not the presence of the dragons, nor their number. It was the quality of their flight.

Sara had thought it remarkable that six shadowbats could form a flock, coordinating their own movements—even when intoxicated, or poisoned—with the movements of their fellows, so that as they ducked and dived and soared and swooped and swerved, looped the loop and curled and whirled themselves into shapes as improbable as their formations, they remained a kind of unit. People, as she had just witnessed, could not organize themselves as economically and as gracefully as that even while they were shuffling about at less than walking pace. Here, though, was a flock whose members must have numbered in the tens of thousands, and whose species must have numbered at least a thousand...and yet they were flocking *together*, maintaining a collective identity as a cloud of clouds: a supercloud as disciplined in its flight and its momentary metamorphoses as a crystal, despite the fact that it was as energetic as a flame.

There was nothing untidy about the astounding legion, however hectic its movement was. It was more orderly than any flicker-winged flock of solid birds. It was more graceful than any multifinned school of silver fish. It was more shapely than the fire fountain in Blackburn's New Town Square.

At first, the dragons flew above the rest of the vaporous host, organizing themselves into a peculiar hierarchy, at whose summit was a single creature larger and more glorious than all the rest—which Sara recognized immediately as an embodiment of the design which had hung in Frank Warburton's shop window for far longer than she had been alive.

It was not long, however, before the flock of dragons merged with the greater flock, to form a company even greater and far more various than their own.

The light and the darkness that danced around one another in a ceaseless ballet as the creatures of brightness mingled with creatures of shadow seemed perfectly natural. The ensemble was dignified in spite of the rapidity with which its components moved, decorous in spite of their delicacy.

Sara remembered how the shadowbats, disturbed by the nectar of her rose, had become even vaguer than artifice had intended, as if they had been attempting to change into something other than bats. None of the individuals in the cloud that soared and streamed above Frank Warburton's monument was drunk, and none was attempting to become something other than it was, but the whole formation seemed to her to be far more than the sum of its parts, in versatility as well as substance. It was only what it was, and yet it held the promise of mysterious changes, the hope of unpredictable progress and metamorphosis.

She knew that it was only vapor. The entire host had no more mass than a storm-cloud—but the vapor was almost alive, and no matter how stupid its individual elements might be, the whole had a kind of intelligence. That intelligence was manifest in the way the cloud played so cleverly and so exuberantly with light and color, and Sara had no doubt at all that it was the Dragon Man's intelligence: the intelligence that had made Frank Warburton a Dragon Man.

It was beautiful, and it was unprecedented. There had never been a display like it in the history of humankind. Given the furious pace at which technology continued to advance, there would probably never be another with quite the same balance of naivety and sophistication. So, at least, Sara was eager to believe. And why should she not be eager to believe it, given that she had known the Dragon Man more intimately, on the last day of his life, than anyone else?

Sara remembered what the Dragon Man had said about her being more aware of the ceaselessness of change than most of his clients, and what he had said about knowing how much he himself had changed, and the extent to which he had lost the sense of being his true self. She wanted to believe that if he had been here, he would have been able to recognize his true self in that marvelous flight of angels, bats and dragons, and know that it had not been lost even though he could no longer embody it.

She took particular care to remember the words that Frank Warburton had regretted having spoken—the words that had revealed more of himself than seemed polite at the time. He had confirmed Father Lemuel's judgment that synthetic organs did not have the same capacity for feeling that real ones did, because biotechnology had not yet progressed to the point at which its practitioners could duplicate the emotional orchestra of hormonal rushes and neural harmonies accurately enough to make the music of real life come out in tune. She wanted to believe that the vast cloud of clouds pirouetting above her head was dancing to the tune of real life, which was coming out absolutely and gloriously right.

It was more illusion than reality, and she knew it, but Sara could see the Dragon Man himself within the cloud, no longer half-dead and half-alive, but complete in life and death alike.

She did not feel in the least ashamed of herself because she could find nothing to say, after three full minutes of the miraculous display, except: "He's here, after all. He is."

She did not feel the need, given that it was so obvious, to add the judgment that the funeral had been anything but pointless.

Nor did she trouble to add the observation that, even though lucky and good would have been entirely the wrong words to use, she was uniquely privileged to be where she was, and who she was, at this particular moment in time.

Afterwards, although it did not seem that an hour had passed, the hummingbirds came. There were thousands of roses on display, hundreds of which must have been designed to generate colibri nectar, but more hummingbirds came to visit Sara's rose than any of the others.

She understood the reason why, and did not want to dispute its adequacy.

She was young.

People wanted to look at her, and welcomed an excuse to do so a little less discreetly than they usually did.

It was a temporary thing, she knew. In a year or two, it would pass. But in the meantime....

She enjoyed every minute, all the more so for knowing that she would be able to renew the sensations, and savor them anew, when she reported to Gennifer everything that she had sensed and felt, within and without.

Mingled with the hummingbirds, always outnumbered but never quite invisible, was a little flock of shadowbats. They moved with more stately precision than the similar flock that had been lured into her bedroom, presumably because they had been given an extra tweak to protect them from the unfortunate side-effects of the tweak that Frank Warburton had improvised. There was, in any case, far too much competition for her nectar to allow them any opportunity for intoxication.

Sara counted the shadowbats twice, having expected that there would be six and being mostly surprised to discover that there were only five. Then she worked out why Mike, when he changed his mind, had not asked the manufacturers to replace the whole set. He had planned a small funeral ceremony of his own for the six lost creatures, deliberately refraining from duplicating the one that she had captured and taken to the Dragon Man's shops.

Compared with the death of a man, the loss of six shadowbats was a very tiny matter—but one that still deserved commemoration.

THE DRAGON MAN, BY BRIAN STABLEFORD

When she caught Mike Rawlinson's eye for one more brief moment, before their respective committees of parents hustled them away, Sara knew that, in spite of their extreme youth, she and he both understood very well what the absence of that sixth shadowbat meant.

It meant that no loss of life was too trivial to be mourned, even—perhaps especially—in a world where humans could legitimately nurse the hope that they, or at least their children, might be capable of living forever.